freefall

BY ARIELA ANHALT

Houghton Mifflin Harcourt
Boston New York

For my mother, Emily Anhalt,
and for my grandmother Marilyn Katz

www.hmhbooks.com

Text set in Garamond No. 3

The Library of Congress has cataloged the hardcover edition as follows:
Freefall/Ariela Anhalt.
p. cm.
Summary: Briar Academy senior Luke prefers avoiding conflict and letting others make his
decisions, but he is compelled to choose whether or not to stand by the best friend whose
reckless behavior has endangered Luke and may have caused another student's death.

[1. Best friends—Fiction. 2. Friendship—Fiction. 3. Peer pressure—Fiction. 4. Boarding
schools—Fiction. 5. Schools—Fiction. 6. Family problems—Fiction. 7. Death—Fiction.
8. Youth writings.] I. Title.
PZ7.A5862Fre 2010
[Fic]—dc22
2009018936

ISBN: 978-0-15-206567-6 hardcover
ISBN: 978-0-547-55216-3 paperback

Manufactured in the United States of America
DOM 10 9 8 7 6 5 4 3 2 1

4500277190

LUKE PRESCOTT stood at the top of the cliff, his toes curled over the edge and pointing downward. Back straight and shoulders relaxed, he let his eyes close peacefully. And he jumped.

A rush of power surged over him. Luke never felt so much in control as when there was none, when all that existed was Luke and the air and the inevitable stop at the end. It was all up to him in those moments. He had decided that he was going to jump and that he was going to land in the water below, and there was absolutely nothing and absolutely nobody that could stop him. He had all the power.

He hit the water with a splash that, months before, had knocked the breath out of him. Now he merely succumbed to the water, letting it close over his head, a stream of bubbles pouring from his mouth and nose as his feet hit the sandy bottom and pushed him to the top. His head broke through the surface of the water, and the solid pounding in his eardrums subsided. He floated on his back, eyes still closed.

His peace was broken just as quickly as it had come over him. "If you keep doing this, you're gonna kill yourself."

Luke turned sharply and choked as he accidentally inhaled what seemed to him like the entire contents of Briar Lake. He coughed, twisted himself around, and began to tread water. He looked up to meet the intruder's eyes and smiled. "Hayden. What are you doing here?"

Hayden stood a few yards away on the bank. He was dressed in his pajamas and a sweatshirt, and his feet were bare. At eighteen, Hayden had the broad-shouldered body of a much older man and the clever, round face of a boy. "I heard you leave," Hayden said, giving Luke a lopsided grin, his ice-blue eyes dancing beneath a mess of dark hair. He reached out a hand to Luke, who paddled over to the edge of the lake.

"I'm fine," Luke said, though the question hadn't been asked. He let Hayden help him out of the water and then collapsed onto the bank. Stretching out on his back, his wet shorts clinging to his skin, Luke shut his eyes again. It wasn't the same. He opened them.

"You should probably stop doing that," Hayden said, nodding toward the cliff. He shuffled his feet awkwardly in the dirt.

Luke grunted noncommittally. *I'm not hurting anyone,* he thought.

"I mean, it's just kinda weird, Luke."

"Yeah, well, I'm kinda weird," Luke said, propping himself up on his elbows.

"Trust me, dude, you're more than kinda weird," said Hayden, squatting down next to Luke.

"Oh, thanks."

Hayden grinned. "You know, I almost broke my nose trying to get here. Tripped over a log, fell flat on my face. Naturally, I blame you for this."

"Naturally," Luke agreed.

"Yep. Totally your fault."

"Of course."

"Couldn't have just been me, you know," Hayden said, leaning conspiratorially toward Luke. "Because everyone knows I'm as graceful as a fucking ballerina."

"Obviously."

"So don't let it happen again."

"Sorry, Hayden. I'll try to do better next time."

"Great. So no more jumping off cliffs in the middle of the night?" Hayden's tone was suddenly serious.

"Come on," Luke said with a short laugh, giving his friend's shoulder a shove. *Drop it, Hayden.*

"Come on, what?" said Hayden. "It's pointless. Why do you keep doing it?"

Luke shrugged. "You wouldn't get it."

"Try me."

I don't want to. "Just let it go," said Luke, annoyance creeping into his voice.

"Is this about—"

"No. "

"Because if—"

"I don't want to talk about that," Luke interrupted, louder than he'd intended.

"Okay. I'm sorry." Hayden looked embarrassed.

Luke sighed. "That has nothing to do with this. I just do this to unwind, to relax."

Hayden stared at him. "You know, I've done it, remember? I've jumped. And I wouldn't exactly call it relaxing."

Luke remembered that night. It had been about a year ago. It was the week before the first fencing meet of the season. He and Hayden and about four other guys had just made varsity on the Briar Academy fencing team. Briar Academy, one of the more elite private schools in California, had many sports teams, but the fencers were the only ones that ever really won anything. Making the team was a pretty big deal.

That night the new varsity members and one of the team captains had gone up to the cliff to jump off. It was a sort of initiation process for the team, and the experience of the jump was treated almost with reverence by the fencers. It wasn't hazing; it was ceremony.

Luke dug his knuckles into the dirt. "I know you have." He exhaled loudly. "Look, I'm tired. Let's head back."

"All right, whatever." Hayden raised his hands defensively. "Have it your way." They both rose up off the bank. "Keep doing it. Break your fucking skull for all I care," Hayden mumbled as Luke padded off to retrieve his clothes from the end of the bank.

They had to sneak back into the dorm quietly so as not to wake any of the resident teachers at the school, who did not particularly like the idea of students wandering off in the middle of the night, especially not off toward the lake. The wooded area around the lake was not visible from the academy, so the students mainly snuck off into the trees to smoke pot or hook up. The school itself was built in a circle formation, with a large green and a commons area at the center. Surrounding that were the dormitory buildings, and encircling them were the academic buildings. The lake hugged the east side of campus, and the woods stretched out from the north side. Through the woods, a five-minute hike and a sharp right turn away, was the cliff.

Luke and Hayden managed to get back into their room unnoticed. Each of the four dormitories had a resident teacher, but luckily the one in Luke's dorm was a particularly sound sleeper. Not that it really would have mattered if they'd been caught; Hayden could talk his way out of anything. He'd smile, crack a joke, make the teacher laugh, and soon he'd be off on his way with simply a warning. If you got caught doing something you shouldn't be doing, Luke figured, Hayden was the guy you wanted with you.

CHAPTER 2

LUKE HAD BREAKFAST every morning with the same group of people. There was Hayden, of course, and Freddy Polk and Drew Devonshire, who were also on the fencing team. Then there was Nicole Johnston, Hayden's girlfriend, and her friend Courtney Chase, who had been hooking up with Drew on and off all year. The group wasn't really exclusive, Luke rationalized. The six of them just got along really well, and other people could sometimes be annoying.

It was a surprise, then, when Luke and Hayden arrived in the dining hall the next morning to see a new face at the table. Luke and Hayden were late, as usual, and from a distance they observed the newcomer as they filled their breakfast trays. Though he was seated, it was still apparent that the new boy was exceptionally tall. His head was low to his tray as he ate, but he looked up when Luke and Hayden arrived, sweeping aside the thick blond hair that rimmed his face. He tossed them a nod. "Hey."

Luke grunted his own greeting, but Hayden was quiet for a moment—not long enough to seem uncertain but long enough to make the boy feel uncomfortable. Hayden did that a lot, Luke noticed, with confident-seeming people. Hayden was very self-assured himself, but it was a quality he appeared to dislike in others. Finally he said, "Hey."

"This is Russell Conrad, the new Jake," introduced Freddy. The substance experimentation of Freddy's old roommate, Jake, had persuaded the administration to suggest he experiment instead with alternative scholastic programs. Freddy had had the double room to himself since November.

Russell smiled blandly. "How's it going?"

"Going good, going good," said Hayden, sliding into the seat next to Nicole and giving her shoulder a nudge. Immediately, Nicole turned and gave him a peck on the cheek. Luke noted this with concern as he sat down. Nicole was not the type to lean on her boyfriend's arm or put her head on his shoulder. She was too proud to behave like one of Hayden's accessories. *She's putting on a show,* he observed. Not wanting to give Hayden time to notice this, Luke said quickly, "So, Russell, where are you from?"

"My family just moved here from Texas," said Russell, returning to his food.

"You don't have an accent," Luke pointed out, and then felt a little stupid.

"Originally from Wisconsin," said Russell, through a mouthful of cereal. He swallowed. "We move around a lot."

"What do you think of Briar?" Luke asked.

Russell smiled again. "Liking it better by the minute." And then, to punctuate the sentence, he glanced at Nicole and sent the smile in her direction.

It was such a bold gesture that, for a moment, everyone at the table was quiet. Nicole pretended indifference. Unfazed, Russell turned to his cereal. Hayden looked at Luke, and Luke shrugged. *I can't believe this guy either.* Hayden turned back to Russell. "So," he said, a tight-lipped smile flickering over his chin, "you just got here?" He asked it like a question, but it was really more of a statement. *You're new. Back off.*

Russell showed no sign that he caught on. "Yep. First day. Getting myself acclimated."

"Russell's a fencer," said Nicole, tucking a stray hair behind her ear. Nicole was jarringly pretty, the kind of pretty that demanded your attention. She and Hayden looked particularly stunning next to each other, both dark haired and light eyed, both with perfect features and confident poses. Luke was halfway convinced that that was the main reason Hayden had gone after her in the first place—they just looked so good together. It couldn't have been for her personality. Nicole was self-absorbed, a little crazy, and sometimes just mean. Like now, when she was clearly giving Hayden and Russell one more thing to be competitive about when she should have been trying to diffuse the situation.

"Oh yeah?" Hayden draped his arm over her shoulder. Nicole leaned into him, but her eyes were on Russell. Hayden rubbed his hand over her arm, and a smirk twitched on Russell's lips, then disappeared. Luke was embarrassed for his friend. *Can't he see he's making an ass of himself? He looks so insecure.*

"I was varsity at my last school," said Russell, although now the polite tone was slipping from his voice. Now he was playing Hayden's game.

"What weapon?" asked Hayden.

"Sabre."

Luke had been so caught up in watching the scene that he hadn't said anything in minutes. Now he was desperately trying to think of ways to break the tension, and he could tell that Courtney, Freddy, and Drew were, too. "That's the same as me and Hayden!" Luke blurted out, too loudly.

Russell gave him an odd look. "Cool."

"Well, we're pretty set for this season," said Hayden. "Luke's been our second for a while now, and Tristan—he's our third—he's pretty tight. I'm our first." Hayden shrugged, a mocking apology. "But hey, we could always use another alternate."

Russell refused to take the bait. He just nodded. "Cool, cool."

Hayden pressed on. "I'm not sure how many bouts you'll get in this season. Usually we toss a few to the JV guys in the last couple meets."

Russell looked up and met Hayden's eyes, and for a moment all the pleasantries and fake smiles were gone, and the two just stared at each other. Both faces were challenging. Luke glanced at Nicole and saw her watching, entranced. He felt disgusted.

Then the bell rang to signal the students to move from the dining hall to their first-period classes. There was an awkward shuffle as Hayden and Russell both looked away, and everyone got to their feet to throw out their leftovers. Russell headed off immediately, as did Courtney, Nicole, and Drew, but as Freddy started to leave, Hayden caught his arm. Luke watched Freddy turn back. "What?"

"Don't bring this tool around again," said Hayden quietly.

Freddy grinned nervously. It was never a good idea to piss off Hayden Applegate. "Yeah. Hey, what a tool, no?"

Hayden grinned back unkindly. "A little bitch."

"Yeah," Freddy agreed. "Seriously."

Hayden turned to Luke, who suddenly felt embarrassed for eavesdropping. Then he realized Hayden was waiting for something. "Yeah," he said, seeing what it was that Hayden wanted. "That kid is an ass." Then Hayden nodded, and Luke and Freddy nodded back at him, and the subject, for the moment, seemed closed.

CHAPTER 3

"MAN," DREW SAID to Luke a few hours later in their fourth-period Spanish class, "that got tense."

Luke nodded. "Yeah. The new guy, what a freak."

"Yeah."

Luke and Drew were sitting in the back of the room. A few yards away, their teacher, Señora Levine, was droning on and on about *las figuras retóricas en el poema,* but they had both tuned her out long ago. Luke liked Drew. He wasn't book smart, but he was smart when it came to getting what he wanted, and he didn't let anyone push him around. Those were qualities Luke respected, qualities he envied.

Drew seemed as unsettled as Luke about what had happened at breakfast. Hayden was rarely so aggressive toward someone he had just met, and the few times in the past that he had been, that someone had always backed off. "Hayden was pissed," Drew said with a forced laugh.

"Can you blame him? I mean, what was wrong with that guy? What was he thinking?"

Drew shrugged. "Guess he was thinking he could get to

Hayden. You guys showed up late, but before that, he was being totally cool. I mean, he hit on Nicole a little bit before you got there, but that's not so bad—I mean, you've seen her."

Luke gave a grunt of agreement. *If I didn't know her, I might actually be attracted to her.*

"Anyway," said Drew, "he was being pretty chill, and then Hayden showed up and Nicole was all over him—which, weird, right?—and, anyway, he just started trying to get under his skin."

"And succeeded," said Luke.

"Hey!" A voice in front of them interrupted the conversation. Luke turned. Rachel Howard, a junior at Briar, was waving a piece of paper in his face. Rachel was petite, with small features and purple hair. Luke liked the purple; it made her unique.

"What?" Luke said, confused. He and Rachel never really talked. They didn't have many friends in common, and she was a year younger.

She rolled her eyes. "Work sheet."

He reddened. "Oh. Sorry. Thanks. Sorry." She stared at him. *Why is she looking at me?*

"You have to take it," she said, slowly, waving the paper in front of him and smiling a little.

Luke could feel his face turn hot. "Right." He tried to laugh. "Yeah." He moved to grab the paper. "Thanks." Drew was snickering next to him. "Shut up!" he hissed.

Rachel frowned. "Excuse me?"

"No, not you!" Luke stammered.

From the front of the room, Señora Levine cleared her throat pointedly. Luke looked around. Everyone was staring at him. He snatched the paper from Rachel's hand. "Sorry," he said. *"Lo siento."*

As Rachel turned away and the class resumed, Luke saw Drew

shaking his head mockingly at him. Luke tried to ignore him and felt like an idiot for the rest of the class.

Hayden was waiting for him outside the door of the classroom when Spanish ended. "Sorry, Drew," Hayden said, pulling Luke away by the arm. "We have a date with the college fairy."

Drew laughed. "Good luck!"

Luke and Hayden had both applied early decision to Dartmouth in November. The fifteenth of December was finally here, and it was time to find out if they'd been accepted. They'd made a plan the day before to skip the first few minutes of lunch and check online together, since the decisions would be up on the college website at noon. *Maybe that's part of why Hayden's been so on edge today*, Luke considered. *Nerves. Stress.* Luke had been trying not to think about Dartmouth since he'd sent in his application.

On the walk back to the dorm room, Hayden actually seemed pretty calm. He was even cheerful. "I feel like this whole waiting period has taken forever, you know? I just want to find out already!"

"Well, you're about to," said Luke. He meant it as an offhand comment, but it came out unkindly.

Hayden looked hurt. "You stressed?"

"No."

"Don't worry. You'll get in."

"I'm not worried about it," Luke insisted.

"Well, then. Aren't we cocky?" Hayden joked. "You should be a little nervous. Fuck, I am."

"Fine, I'm nervous. Happy?"

Hayden raised an eyebrow. "Jesus. Is this about break?"

Yes. "No."

"Are you going to go home tomorrow?"

"Just for the weekend. My mom's trying to get together some kind of early holiday dinner or something." Luke's family didn't usually make a big deal out of holidays, particularly in recent years; it had been hard to feel celebratory.

"That could be fun."

Are you kidding? "Yeah."

Hayden laughed and shoved Luke in the shoulder. "You look like you're on death row. You're just going home, Luke. You'll get some sleep, eat food, see your family. Won't be so bad."

You don't know my family. "I guess so."

"Come on," Hayden said as they reached the dorm room. "Chin up or whatever. Show some holiday spirit." He put on a cheesy smile, and Luke had to laugh.

"All right," Luke said with a sigh. "Let's do this."

They logged onto their computers, and the room was suddenly quiet. Luke went through the online steps. College website, admissions, student identification, undergraduate prematriculation menu, admissions decision. "Mr. Prescott, we are sorry to inform you—" He stopped reading.

He was suddenly aware that Hayden was laughing next to him. "Mr. Applegate!" Hayden crowed. "Congratulations! We are pleased to inform you that your application to Dartmouth College has been accepted!" Hayden pumped his fist in the air. "Yes!" Then, looking a little sheepish, he turned to look at Luke. "Sorry. Uh, how about you?"

Luke stared at his computer screen. "It's not working," he said. It was the first thing that came to his mind. He closed the computer window. "It says my password's wrong."

"Shit, that sucks!" said Hayden. "Try again."

"I tried a couple times," said Luke. "I think I'm gonna call later."

Hayden moved toward Luke's computer. "Here, let me—"

"No! I mean, it's fine. I've tried a bunch of times, so I'm just gonna call."

Hayden gave him a strange look. "Okay . . ."

"There's a number on the site. So I'll call. You should go to lunch. Spread the good news." He felt like crying.

Hayden frowned. "I mean, I can wait with you." Luke could see the empty offer weighing on Hayden's shoulders.

Luke forced a smile. "No. Seriously, go. Celebrate. Congratulations."

Hayden grinned broadly. "Thanks! Oh man! This is sweet! And you're gonna get in, too. I can feel it. Seriously, I have like a sixth sense about this shit."

"Great," Luke said, with irony that sailed over Hayden's head.

"All right, but we'll talk later, yeah?" Hayden headed for the door. "Like, come find me at lunch or something, okay?"

Luke swallowed. "Yeah. Definitely." And Hayden was gone.

College website, admissions, student identification, undergraduate prematriculation menu, admissions decision, we are sorry to inform you. Luke went through the steps again, just to be sure. It was over. He shut down his computer, closed his eyes, and lay his head down on top of it. *Perfect,* he thought. *Everything is just perfect.*

Hours later, when Hayden came back to the room, Luke was sound asleep on the desk. "Hey, Luke, are you awake?"

I am now . . .

Hayden didn't wait for a response. "I need to talk to you about something."

"What time is it?" Luke asked groggily.

"Four." Hayden sat down on his bed, noticing Luke's eyes were still squeezed shut. He stuck out a long leg and kicked Luke's desk chair. "Come on, get up, it's important."

"Four in the afternoon?" Luke had slept through all of his afternoon classes.

"Yeah, Luke, focus."

With great effort, Luke pulled his head off the desk and turned around to look at Hayden. "Okay, I'm awake. What's going on?"

"Nicole and I broke up."

Luke was awake. "What? When?"

"Like an hour ago. I've been walking around campus."

"Why'd you break up with her?"

"No," Hayden said angrily. "*She* broke up with *me*. Can you believe it? She said I don't pay enough *attention* to her. I mean, what the fuck, Luke?"

Luke sighed. *I don't want to deal with this now.* "Maybe it's a good thing."

"What? How?" Hayden asked, his voice an octave too high.

"Well—"

"You just don't like her. But you could think about me for a second! This sucks! It's going to wreck my whole vacation!"

Rubbing his eyes, Luke stood and sat down on his own bed across from his friend. Time to stroke Hayden's ego. "No, it won't. Your vacation is going to be ten times better without having to deal with her. She screwed up her own vacation. She's probably already wishing she hadn't broken up with you."

Hayden flopped back on the bed. "You think?"

"Yeah," Luke said. "And you don't need her, anyway."

"Yeah." Hayden sat up. "I mean, it's not like I need that slut. I can do whatever I want now."

"Damn straight." Luke leaned over on his side and shut his eyes.

"Hey, Luke?"

Luke groaned. "What?"

"You think this has anything to do with that new kid?"

He didn't open his eyes. "Jesus, Hayden."

"What? You think it does?"

Luke sat up. "Would you just give it a rest?"

"Come on, Luke, can't you see this is important?"

"Important?" Luke said incredulously, standing up in frustration. "*Important?* Your girlfriend dumped you. Oh, how terrible it must be to be you!"

"What the hell, man?"

"You know, some people have real problems. Some people have actual things to deal with."

"What the fuck is the matter with you?"

"Nothing! I'm just sick of your complaining."

"Fuck you! I don't need this!" Hayden spat out, standing up and heading for the door.

"Then what are you keeping me up for?" Luke shouted back.

"Go to hell," Hayden said, and left, slamming the door behind him.

Luke sat back down on the bed in the now-silent room. "Damn it," he whispered.

CHAPTER 4

THE TRAIN from Forest County to Springfield took two hours. Luke spent most of that time kicking himself over what he'd said to Hayden. *He probably hates my guts by now.* He tried looking out the window as the train rattled along, but he didn't see anything interesting enough to distract him. Just a bunch of trees and run-down houses and fractured bits of sky in between.

Eventually, Luke's train slowed to a stop and pulled into the station. The train station in Springfield, California, wasn't actually so much of a station as a rickety wooden platform with rotted stairs leading down into a small parking lot in the middle of nowhere. Luke shouldered his backpack, stepped out onto the platform, and gazed down at the lot. His mother's car was parked in the shade of an overgrown shrub. He headed toward it slowly, taking a few deep breaths and bracing himself.

She got out of the car as he approached, giving him a tentative little wave. "Hey there." She was a small woman, very thin, with bottle-blond hair and a generically pretty face. She was dressed nicely in a soft blue sweater and beige pants. It bothered Luke that she looked so put together, so normal. But of course, he reminded himself, it was how she always looked.

His whole body had tensed up as soon as he'd caught sight of her. "Mom." He tried to greet her politely enough, but he could see the disappointed look on her face as they both got into the car.

"Was the trip long?" she asked as they pulled out of the lot.

"No," Luke said, wishing he'd stayed at school.

She nodded, tapping her fingers on the steering wheel. "Well, everyone's so excited to see you. Your aunt and uncle are coming for dinner."

"Cool." He didn't want to sit here with her and make conversation like this, as if everything was perfectly normal between them.

"So, of course you'll want to change before then," she said, looking at his jeans and sweatshirt.

"Yeah."

"Or, well, you don't *have* to," she clarified, her face flushing. "I mean, I just thought you might want to. Or it might be nice." He stared at her. "Well, you can, um . . . you can decide."

"Okay."

"And I've been cooking all day, been really busy, so hopefully . . ." She coughed. "And, uh . . ."

Thirty seconds and she's already run out of things to say to me. "Is Jason at home?" he asked.

"Actually, I think he went out to see some friends today, but he'll be back later this afternoon."

"Cool."

"Well, listen, I want to hear all about school," she said, turning to smile at him. "Tell me everything."

Tell me everything. It was a little funny, Luke figured, her saying that now. Acting like she wanted to know. Acting like she had any right to know. *You gave that up a long time ago.* "School's good," he told her, shifting his body so that he was angled toward the window.

"And how's . . . how's fencing?" she scrambled. "Your season's just starting, isn't it? That must be exciting."

"Yep."

He heard her sigh. "Luke."

"What?"

There was a pause. "I was thinking maybe tomorrow we could go see a movie. Is there something you want to see?"

With you? No. He shrugged.

"Or we could rent one."

"Whichever," he muttered. She was making him a little queasy.

"Um, well, you let me know."

He hated the way she was guilt-tripping him. Making him feel like the bad guy. He had shown up, hadn't he? He had said hello, talked to her. He hadn't owed her that.

After a few more minutes of uncomfortable silence, the car arrived at 119 Sycamore Street, Springfield, California. Luke had had to memorize that address on his first day of kindergarten. His teacher, Ms. Jacobs, had made them all learn their addresses. *Everything was simpler in kindergarten,* Luke thought. He remembered it all so much more clearly than he did the past few years. There were images, but no real clarity. A handgun, a phone call, a siren. Nothing made all that much sense anymore.

The large house somehow managed to seem both welcoming and imposing at once. A string of Christmas lights hung on the doorway, and Luke smiled vaguely looking at them. A neighbor or passerby would have thought they had been put up for the holiday season, and indeed they had. Four years ago. It had taken Luke's father a whole day of work, a whole day of endless profanities, to hang up the lights, and after he did, he vowed never to have anything to do with them again. Unfortunately, to the humiliation of the rest of the family during the summer months, this included taking them down.

A memory appeared unexpectedly in Luke's mind. It was a little over three years ago, and Luke, a gawky freshman who had not yet had his braces removed, was standing next to his brother in the office of Headmaster Grunberg. "Boys," the frail old man rasped, pushing his glasses farther up on his nose, "I'm sorry to have to tell you this." *I'm sorry to have to tell you this. I'm sorry to have to tell you this.*

Then, just as quickly as the memory had appeared, it vanished. The car came to a stop in the driveway, and Luke got out immediately. His mother followed, standing by awkwardly as he got his backpack out of the trunk. "You'll probably want to unpack," she said. "Well, I see you didn't bring very much."

Luke shrugged. "Not staying that long."

"Right. Sure. Well. You'll probably still want to . . . settle in."

"Yeah."

"Jason could be back any minute."

"You said."

"Right." She pushed a stiff strand of hair behind her ear. "Are you hungry?" she asked.

"No, thanks," he mumbled, and jerked away toward the house. He hated being here. It was making him remember things he didn't like to.

He entered the house ahead of his mother and almost bolted up the winding staircase up to his room. *She hasn't moved anything. Good.* Although Luke didn't really like being in his house anymore, he still liked his bedroom. It reminded him of being younger, of things being simpler and safer. Sitting on his bed, just where he'd left it at the end of the long, painful summer at home, was the giant stuffed ostrich his parents had bought him for his seventh birthday. (Luke was still sort of attached to "Ned," but there was no way he'd be caught dead with it at school.) Next to the door were the three-foot-tall Power Ranger stickers Luke had put up when he was little and couldn't take down without damaging the wall. Over the bed hung a picture of Charlie Parker.

It was his father who'd gotten him into jazz. When he was ten, his dad had gotten him a CD of Miles Davis. He'd been skeptical, but finally he'd inserted it into his CD player. Luke had loved the tone and had listened to it over and over for hours on end. He started buying CDs by himself, Stan Getz and Ben Webster and Joe Lovano. He preferred the pure saxophone to the saxophones with accompanists or pianos or anything that masked the true sound. Then, one day, Luke heard Charlie Parker, and he'd never been able to listen to jazz the same way again. Luke looked at the poster, reached up, tore it from the wall, and tossed it into the wastebasket. He hadn't listened to jazz in years.

A few minutes later, Luke heard a car pull up outside. Jason was home. Luke went downstairs and arrived in the foyer just as his brother reached the front door. Jason loped in and shut the door behind him. He smiled when he saw Luke. "Hey," he said, stuffing his hands in his pockets and hunching his shoulders a little.

He was a couple of inches shorter than Luke, more compact and muscled.

"Hey," Luke said, feeling, as he always did around his brother, like a string bean.

"How you been?"

"Okay. You?"

"I've been good. Yeah, I've been good." Luke and Jason eyed each other with the polite awkwardness of brothers who were never as close as they thought they should have been. Jason's face flushed a little. "You know, school, it's tough, but I'm doing okay. Briar still surviving without me?" he joked.

"Yeah," Luke said.

"You hear back from Dartmouth yet?"

"No, not yet," Luke lied. *How long can I deflect these questions?*

"Kind of late, no? I mean, I think I'd already found out by this time last year."

Luke shrugged. "I guess."

Jason nodded. There was an uncomfortable pause. Luke tried to think of something to say. Jason appeared to be doing the same thing. *It shouldn't be this difficult.*

Jason rocked back on his heels. "Weird being back here, huh?" he said, not meeting Luke's eyes. It had been awhile since Jason had been home; he'd done an internship in Seattle over the summer.

"I guess." Suddenly, Luke couldn't get away fast enough. "I've still got some unpacking to do, so I'll see you later."

"All right," Jason said, and Luke went back upstairs.

He meant to go to his room, but somehow he wound up in his parents'. He still thought of it that way, his parents' room, even though it was only his mother's now. The room looked pretty much the same, except that on the left side of the bed, where Luke's father had slept, there sat a small stack of books. Luke stared at it. Those books didn't belong on that bed. His father belonged there. He crossed the room quickly and pushed the books onto the carpet.

As soon as he did it, he felt embarrassed. *Why should it matter to me, anyway?* He knelt and picked up the books, restacking them on the bed. *It's her bed. She can put whatever she wants on it.* He stepped back and took a look at the stack, trying to decide if his mother would notice he'd disturbed it.

His stomach lurched. He had restacked the books, he realized, in order of size, with the bindings of the books perfectly aligned. The stack was precise. It was flawless. He swallowed hard, took a deep breath, and left the room.

Don't think about it. Do not think about it.

He returned to his bedroom and closed the door behind him. It was three fifteen. Dinner would be at five thirty. It was always at five thirty. Luke's father used to joke that in the event that one of the clocks should break and stop at five twenty-nine, they'd have to wait until it could be fixed so that it could read five thirty before they sat down at the table. But Luke's mother liked that, the punctuality, so Luke and his brother and father had always humored her.

Luke put on a button-down shirt and changed from his jeans into the wrinkled pair of khakis he had brought. Dressed and ready, he had no idea what to do with himself for the next two hours. He opened his desk drawer and looked through its contents. There were some old papers, a broken calculator, a photo album. Curious, he opened the album.

It was of a fishing trip he'd taken with his family the summer when he was nine. They'd all made the long plane trip to New Hampshire because Luke's mother's boss had offered them his family's house over there for a couple of weeks to celebrate her promotion. His mother must have taken the pictures, because she wasn't in any of them. They were all of one day out on the lake. Jason, age ten, thrilled at catching a fish. Jason putting the fish into a bucket. Luke stealthily picking up the fish and tossing it back in the water. Jason shoving Luke into the water. Dad laughing.

Flipping through the pages, Luke couldn't help feeling like he was looking down on a family he didn't know, that he wasn't a part of. The little blond boy with the crooked front teeth was not him. It was some other kid with a perfect, happy family. Not him.

He stopped at the picture of the laughing man. Luke's eyes narrowed. The man was leaning back on the dock, watching as one son splashed in the water, the other standing next to him. The man looked happy. Luke felt hatred. He closed the album.

CHAPTER 5

AS SOON AS Uncle Lou and Aunt Patricia arrived for dinner, Luke's mother navigated her way out of a sea of papers and ushered them all into the living room. Uncle Lou, Luke's mother's brother, was a ridiculously fat man who spoke very little. His wife, Aunt Patricia, was a ridiculously thin woman who spoke very much. Luke had never really gotten to know either of them, as they showed up only for holidays, but he always dreaded their visits. Luke's mother and Aunt Patricia often had trouble being in the same room together.

Luke's mother settled herself into an armchair while her brother and sister-in-law sat stiffly on a couch and Jason slumped down into a second armchair. Luke entered the room last and, seeing that the only seat left was next to his Aunt Patricia on the couch, perched himself on the piano bench.

"How was your drive up?" Luke's mother asked, playing hostess.

"Fine," answered Uncle Lou.

"Oh, he's just being kind," broke in Aunt Patricia. "It was awful, actually. Terrible traffic."

Luke and Jason rolled their eyes at each other. *Here we go again.*

"They're doing some work on the highway," Luke's mother explained.

"It seems like this area is constantly under construction," said Aunt Patricia. "There was so much traffic on the way up."

"There's a train," Luke's mother said crisply.

Uncle Lou cleared his throat, trying to diffuse the tension. "Yes, well. Luke, Jason, how is school?"

"Fine," both brothers said automatically.

"And how's work, Meredith?" he asked.

"Good," she said, smiling. "Busy, but good."

"I don't know how you do it," Aunt Patricia said sweetly. "Balancing your career and your family."

"Well, I try," said Luke's mother guardedly.

"It must be hard on your boys, though," said Aunt Patricia.

"Well—" Luke's mother started.

"And of course it was hard on Jack," Aunt Patricia interrupted. Uncle Lou winced.

Luke saw his mother's jaw clench. "We really don't mind," he jumped in, feeling a strange urge to defend her. He locked eyes with his aunt. "We're very proud of her."

Luke's mother looked at him, a little shocked.

"Uh, yeah. Proud," said Jason, sitting up a little in his chair and sending Luke a small, slightly startled glance.

"Well," said Aunt Patricia, sounding a little miffed, "isn't that sweet." She forced a smile. "Such good boys. Their father would be so proud. Such a pity."

Luke's mother beamed aggressively back at Aunt Patricia. It

looked to Luke like a war of smiles, with each woman trying to outdo the other. "I'm sure he would be."

"Just *awful* what happened," Aunt Patricia said. "Just *awful*."

Luke's mother gave a little cough. "Yes, well, Patricia, that was three years ago." Her smile was beginning to waver. Luke was disappointed. He was rooting for her.

"Of course. Probably hurts to think about," Aunt Patricia pressed. "I mean, when you think about what would make—"

"Patricia," Uncle Lou broke in.

"No, it's all right, Lou," Luke's mother said. "Patricia can say whatever she wants. We'll leave tact behind tonight, then, won't we?" Aunt Patricia gave an alarmed little laugh. "Now, who's hungry?"

They all filed into the dining room and sat down around the table. A giant roast beef was set at the front of the table, next to a large casserole of potatoes au gratin and another of green beans swimming in almonds and butter. Luke's mother glowed, obviously pleased by how it all looked. "Will you carve, Lou?" she asked her brother.

Uncle Lou began to stand, but Aunt Patricia put her hand on his arm. "Oh, Meredith, I'm so sorry, but this really isn't good for Lou's diet."

Luke's mother raised an eyebrow. "His diet?"

"Well, he's been trying to lose a few since Thanksgiving, and really, this . . ." Aunt Patricia gestured toward the table.

"Now, Patricia—" began Uncle Lou, eyeing the roast.

"Lou, do you really want to undo all the work you've done with one meal?" asked Aunt Patricia. "Of course you don't," she answered. "I'm sorry, Meredith, this really won't do. Lou is on a very strict diet. Low carbohydrates and low fat." She looked pointedly at her sister-in-law. "You really ought to try it."

Meredith Prescott swallowed, her throat muscles twitching visibly.

"Maybe we have something in the kitchen!" Luke blurted out. "Um, I'll go see." He half walked and half ran to the kitchen, relieved to be able to break away from the tension of the dining room.

Just as Luke began to look aimlessly around the huge kitchen for anything remotely resembling health food, the door swung open, and Jason stepped in. "Hey. How's it going?"

Luke reddened. "I'm not exactly sure . . ."

Jason laughed. "I wouldn't worry about it. I think Uncle Lou's decided the roast's made of a meatlike vegetable substance, because he's already eaten like half of it while they've been arguing."

Luke laughed. "God, they're something, aren't they?"

"Yeah, for a second there I thought Mom was going to go kung fu on Aunt Patricia." Jason grinned. "That would've been something to see."

"Yeah."

"You hungry?"

Luke shrugged. "Not really."

Jason nodded back at the dining room. "It looks like they'll be awhile. Want to sneak out for a bit?"

"Yeah, why not. Not like they'll notice we're gone." He meant it as a joke, but once he said it, he realized it didn't sound too funny.

Luke and Jason stepped out onto the screened-in porch that branched out from the kitchen. They leaned back against the house, staring out at the backyard. Jason reached into his back pocket and pulled out a pack of cigarettes. He offered it to Luke. "Want one?"

"No, I'm good."

Jason lit a cigarette and inhaled deeply. He closed his eyes and breathed out, a stream of smoke pouring from his nostrils. He turned and saw Luke looking at him. "What?"

"No, I just—I didn't know you smoked."

Jason shrugged. "Helps me relax."

"Oh. You probably shouldn't, though."

"Thanks a lot, Mr. Surgeon General." Jason brought the cigarette back to his lips.

"I'm just saying, you know, it's not so . . . healthy. People get, like, addicted."

"Oh, shut up. I don't need a lecture from you, too, Luke," Jason snapped. "I get enough of that at school."

"What are you talking about?" Luke asked, more out of curiosity than concern.

Jason tapped a heel against the side of the house. "I just didn't do too well this semester."

"Nah, I'm sure you did fine."

"I've been asked not to come back after the break."

"Oh."

"Yeah."

"How come you, uh . . ." Luke didn't know how to ask the question, so he just stopped.

Jason looked down. "College just wasn't what I expected. There was so much we were supposed to already know and I didn't. So it was so much easier to, you know, blow it off."

"You tell her yet?" Luke asked, nodding toward the house.

"Not yet."

"You gonna?"

"Yeah. I guess I have to, don't I?" Jason smiled. "That'll be a fun conversation."

"I bet."

Jason sighed. "She's gonna be upset."

"Uh-huh."

"I just feel bad. Putting it on her." Jason paused. "And then, you know, it's like another thing she's gotta tell people. Like, when they ask about you and me."

"Yeah," Luke said snidely. "I bet that'll be the very first thing on her mind."

"Well, that's not what I meant. I didn't mean it would be the *first* thing." Jason winced. "All I'm saying is I know she's going to feel upset, and I feel . . . bad," he finished lamely.

"Don't. She wouldn't if the situation was reversed."

Jason's mouth twitched. "You mean if Mom got kicked out of Stanford?"

"No," Luke said, failing to keep his voice even. "I mean if Mom had something she had to tell you that was going to hurt you, she probably wouldn't be so worried about how to tell you. About how's the nicest way to tell you."

Jason put up a hand. "Don't."

"Fine." Luke looked away. "Anyway, it's not like she's going to cry about it. She'll probably just be pissed. Yell. Whatever."

"Actually," Jason said slowly, "you know, she's mellowed out a lot. I mean, she's still . . . a little uptight, maybe . . . but really, she's trying." He eyed Luke hesitantly. "You could try a little, too, you know."

"Thanks for letting me know," Luke responded, his voice cold.

"All I mean is that you might be happier if you just let this go. It's so much easier that way. Being angry is exhausting, you know? And me, I just couldn't do it anymore."

Luke exhaled slowly into one hand. "If you can forgive her for what she did, then fine. I can't."

There was a pause. Jason looked away. "Yeah. Well. Anyway, I'm going to tell her soon. I mean, not right away but, like, when the moment's right."

"Oh. So what are you going to do now?"

"I don't know."

"Are you going to apply somewhere else?"

Jason rolled his eyes. "I don't know, Luke. What school's going to accept me if I've been kicked out of Stanford in my first year? I mean, come on, I've got to be realistic."

"So what, then? Are you going to get a job?"

"As what?"

"I don't know. You have to do something, don't you?"

He shrugged apathetically. "I guess I'll stick around here for a little while. Stanford'll let me come back if I skip two terms. So maybe I'll wait."

"Wait here?"

"I don't know yet."

"Don't you need, like, a plan?"

"Yeah." Jason hunched his shoulders and stared down at his feet. "Well, I'll make one. I got time, though. I got a lot of time now."

"Oh. Okay." Luke tried to think of the right thing to say. "That sucks."

"Yep." Luke's brother took another drag on his cigarette. "But I guess I won't have to take those finals everyone's been stressing about." He started to laugh, and it turned into a throaty cough.

Luke stood up. "I'm going to go back in. They're probably wondering where we are by now."

"Okay," Jason said.

"You coming?"

"In a bit," Jason said, bringing his cigarette up to his lips once again.

Luke looked back over his shoulder at his brother. "You have to tell her soon, Jason."

"I will," he said, rubbing the top of his head with his hand. The burning end of the cigarette skated dangerously over Jason's crew cut. "Not tonight, though. Maybe tomorrow."

"Yeah," Luke said, and for a moment, standing there on the porch, both brothers actually believed that Jason would.

CHAPTER 6

"YOU KNOW, you don't have to leave this afternoon," Luke's mother told him over breakfast. They were sitting in the kitchen, eating the scrambled eggs she'd made. Jason was still asleep, so it was just the two of them. "I know we'd agreed you'd come back for the weekend, but it just feels a little silly, doesn't it? I mean, it really comes out to be just over a day."

"I guess," he mumbled, stuffing his mouth with eggs. *I will not stay here with you. Not any longer than I have to. Don't even try it.*

"But maybe you have things you want to get back to," she said quickly. "That's all right. That's good."

"Yeah."

She nodded. "Okay. Well, I was thinking maybe this afternoon we could—"

"I'm kind of tired," he said, cutting her off.

"All day?"

He hated the way she said that, like it was more of an accusation than a question. "Yeah," he answered. "All day."

"Okay," his mother said. "I'm sorry. I don't mean to push you."

She shrugged. "But you do make me walk on eggshells, don't you? No, I don't want to fight. I'm sorry." Another pause. "I actually wanted to talk to you."

"About what?" he asked warily.

She had a strange expression on her face, like she was making a decision. "Well, what Patricia said. About your dad. I wasn't sure if it upset you."

"Oh," he said, his appetite fading. He wished he'd never come downstairs this morning. "It didn't."

"She's pretty tactless, isn't she?"

"Guess so," Luke answered noncommittally.

"I don't know what Lou . . ." His mother sighed. "Anyway. Since she brought it up, I just wanted to make sure you were all right."

"Yeah, well, like I said, it didn't bother me, so . . ." *Let it go.*

"Okay," she said. "Because if there was anything you wanted to talk about, I just want you to know that I'm here."

You're here. Fantastic. "Don't you think it's a little late for that?" he asked her before he could stop himself.

There was a moment of total quiet. Then, "We could talk about that, if you'd like."

I should just leave. I should walk away before she says anything else.

She leaned forward across the table. "Look, I know that I didn't . . . say the right things, do the right things, after he died. I know that. But I was in a really rough place right then."

Luke didn't want to listen to any more of her excuses. It didn't make any difference. He'd heard them before. They didn't change anything.

"I don't even remember the week after it happened," she told him.

I'm not doing this. I'm not hearing this. He started to stand.

"I'm trying to explain," she said, taking hold of his elbow. "Would you let me explain?"

He shook her off. "What's to explain? You don't remember. Isn't that nice for you? *I* remember."

"I know you do. I'm just trying to say I wasn't completely—"

He sat back down and looked her right in the eye. "I remember having to hear about it from someone I barely knew. I remember not even being able to reach you on the phone for days after. I remember coming home for the funeral and you not even *looking* at me. So maybe you don't remember, but I remember very well." He stood again.

"Luke—"

But he didn't want to hear what she had to say, so he kept talking. "Do you know what that was like for me? It was his funeral, and he was gone, and I was bawling, and you wouldn't even look at me."

She wasn't looking at him now. She was looking down at the table.

"I called home so many times. I didn't believe the headmaster when he told me. I thought, no way, if this had happened, you would tell me yourself. You wouldn't send a message. It wasn't the kind of thing you could send in a message." He gritted his teeth. "So I called you. Jason and I, we both called. Over and over. Waiting for you to answer the phone and tell us what was going on." He stared at the side of her head, waiting for her to turn and meet his eyes.

Finally, she did. "You're right," she said. "Okay? Is that what you want to hear? I agree with you. But we have to get past this, you and I."

No, actually. We really don't.

"And I get that this is probably some sort of outlet for you. Maybe it's easier for you to hate me than him—"

"Do not analyze me!" he said, almost shouting it.

His mother shook her head. "God, you're tough."

Luke rolled his eyes. "Yes, this is on me, isn't it? This is all my fault."

"Well, you're certainly not making it any easier," she said. "You're not the only one who lost him. I know that I shut you out, and I know that it was horrible. I'm not perfect, okay?"

"Whatever." He started to walk away.

"You know, your brother understands this," she called after him.

He turned abruptly. "Oh, does he? He forgives you, Mom, is that what you think?" He laughed. "Jason doesn't forgive you; he's just tired of being mad at you. He's not sympathetic; he's lazy."

"Don't say that."

"Why not?" Luke fired back, not even thinking of the words as they left his lips. "He is. He's lazy. He's weak. Just like Dad."

She looked like she wanted to hit him. "Get out of my kitchen."

"Gladly." He left the kitchen on unsteady feet and went to his room. He shut the door behind him and lay down on his bed and buried his face in the pillow. He did not cry. He pushed his forehead farther and farther into the pillow, forcing the feathers aside until he could feel the wood of his headboard pressing through the fabric. It hurt, and Luke pressed harder. He didn't want to think. He didn't want anything. He hid out in his room all day.

In the afternoon a taxi arrived in the driveway, and Luke assumed it was his ride. *Well, good. It's not like I wanted her to drive me to the station.* He lugged his backpack down the flight of stairs to where Jason and his mother waited in the living room. Jason was reading a copy of *Sports Illustrated,* and his mother was sorting brown folders on the coffee table. Neither of them saw him come in at first, but finally Jason looked up to see him standing in the doorway. "Oh, hey, Luke."

"Hey. Think my ride's here." He looked to his mother for confirmation, but her face was unreadable.

Jason stood. "I guess I'll see you soon, right?"

"Yeah," Luke said. "Yeah, I'll give you a call at New Year's."

"Okay."

Luke's mother walked over. "Have a good trip back," she said, as if nothing had happened that morning.

Fine. "Yeah, I will."

He gave his brother a quick hug and turned awkwardly toward his mother. He stared at her a second, then turned away. "Well," he said, shouldering his bag. "I'd better go." In a few moments, he was seated in a taxicab outside 119 Sycamore Street. He looked out the window to see his mother and brother through the living room window. And shortly after, Luke was pulling away.

CHAPTER 7

LUKE ALWAYS FELT strange returning to school after a break. Everything felt out of place, like even the air was wrong. When he got back to Briar after the weekend at home, he spent a few hours trying to readjust. It had been such a draining couple of days that Luke had no energy to do anything productive. He lazed about, reading and playing pinball on his computer, bored out of his mind but too tired to get up and go anywhere.

After losing what must have been his one millionth game against the computer, Luke glanced over at Hayden's side of the room. The bed was unmade and a pillow lay on the floor. He resisted the compulsive urge to pick up the pillow and set it back on the bed. *Obsessive.* He stayed seated on his own bed with his computer in his lap, waiting for the feeling of comfort to kick in. When it didn't, he left.

Luke headed away from the dorm, not quite in control of where he was going but aware of where he knew his feet would eventually carry him. Outside, the campus was reverently silent, as most of the students were still gone. It had rained overnight, and cold puddles of brown water pooled along the sides of the pathways, claiming the soil as their own. Luke made a point of stepping in each one, watching the dirt float upward to the surface as the muddy water slowly seeped through the tops of his shoes and into his socks.

And, of course, he ended up where he'd always thought he would, standing at the rocky foot of the cliff, the bushes brushing up against his legs, the cloudy sky's reflection darkening the surface of the lake. He stuck a soggy sneaker into the water. The rain had made it cold, but Luke didn't hesitate. He twisted back to the wall of the cliff and stuck his foot in the first foothold. He climbed.

From the top, the entire expanse of Briar Lake was visible, but Luke didn't pause to take in the view. He didn't stop to take off his jeans and shirt or his muddy shoes. He didn't wait to judge his leap so as to not land too close to the rocks that lay below. He just jumped, no running start, no moment of preparation.

The water was even colder than he'd expected, and he shivered when he came to the surface, just a few feet from the pointed rocks. A lock of his hair drifted forward across his field of vision, and Luke ducked underwater to brush it away. He felt the cold water wash over his head, trickle into his ears, and press his wet clothes against him. His ears started to ring, and his chest told him he needed to come up for air. He waited for his feet to push him up from the bottom. They didn't. His throat was beginning to burn, and his eyes, unaccustomed to being open underwater, were starting to drift shut on their own. All he had to do was wait. And it would be easy. So very easy.

With a roar that came out as a powerful stream of bubbles, Luke shoved his feet against the bottom of the lake with such force that he was sure his legs would be sore afterward. The water rushed by him like a strong wind, and he smashed loudly through the surface, propelling his body nearly totally out of the water.

He couldn't get out of the lake fast enough. He flopped facedown on the bank, barely noticing the sand that clung to his wet clothes and pricked his face. He'd inhaled a lot of water, and for a few minutes he was soothed by the sound of his own hacking cough. But when it was gone, he was left there, lying on the bank, his body trembling from what he told himself was the cold.

After a moment Luke stood, taking in a few shaky breaths. He swallowed painfully and rubbed his hand across the back of his slippery neck, wondering how long he'd been under. It had seemed like forever, but it couldn't have been too long. Maybe only seconds.

He shuddered once again, and this time he knew that it wasn't from the cold. *I am not my father.* "I am not my father!" he shouted to the water, which paid him no mind and continued its perpetual journey around the lake.

He wished he'd never gone home. Everything was easier when he just stayed away. *Maybe,* he considered, *I will never go home again.* It was so unfair. Everyone else got to go home and be happy. Everyone else was probably loving the break right now, relaxing with their perfect little families.

Luke had no idea there was another student still at Briar Academy until, a few days later, he was practicing his fencing footwork at three o'clock in the morning and heard an angry shout from the room below. "Hey! Shut up! I'm trying to sleep down here!"

Luke stopped abruptly, his socks sliding on the floor. "Sorry!" he called down. "I didn't realize—"

"Whatever, just shut up!"

Though irritated, Luke obliged and went back to bed, racking his brain to figure out who else was still at Briar. He hadn't recognized the voice, and he couldn't remember who had the room below him. Who else was still there? It bugged him that he couldn't remember. Then it hit him. Cooper Albright.

Cooper Albright was a senior. Yet, despite his having spent almost four years at Briar, there were very few people at the school who actually knew him. There were, however, a great many people who knew *of* him. No one was really sure how Cooper did it, but he always seemed to have his hands on copious amounts of pot, LSD, crack, even the random stuff like opium. Luke personally had never bought anything from him, but he knew a fair amount of people who had. Most of them thought that Cooper was annoying, but since the stuff he got was hard to come by at the isolated school, Cooper was tolerated by the student body. Luke was a bit uncertain about going to see him, but Cooper was the only one there, and though he hated to admit it, Luke was getting a little lonely. So the next morning, Luke went downstairs and knocked on the door of Cooper's room.

"It's unlocked!" came a shout from within.

Cautiously, Luke went inside. The room was dark. Impulsively, Luke reached for the light switch. "Don't touch that. No light," Cooper said, his voice coming from under a pile of clothes on the bed.

"All right . . ." Luke looked around, realizing he was standing in, without a doubt, the messiest room he'd ever seen. It was even worse than Hayden's half of the room the two of them shared. As his eyes adjusted to the lack of light, Luke was able to appreciate the sheer awesomeness of Cooper's trashed dorm room. Tall mountains of dirty clothes and other things that might have at one point been recognizable littered the floor. The walls were covered in multi-colored stains, and a heavy, sweet-smelling mist hung in the air. Luke wasn't sure what it was, but he was willing to bet it wasn't shortbread.

Cooper poked his head up from the pile of clothes. His pale, shaved scalp and bloodshot eyes were barely visible in the dark. He grinned. "I guess your parents don't want anything to do with you either."

"*Excuse* me?" It wasn't the statement that bothered Luke so much as the way that Cooper said it, like it was a fact, a declaration, a universal piece of knowledge.

Cooper just laughed. He stood up, the clothes falling to the floor. The kid was scarily thin, practically two-dimensional. He was short, with an elfin face, leering green eyes, and an unfortunately shaped nose. He leaned forward toward Luke conspiratorially, his voice turning into a hoarse, raspy whisper. "What are you doing here?"

Luke took a step back, disgusted. "I just wanted to see who was home already."

"Home," Cooper mused. "That's interesting."

"You know what I mean." *What am I doing here?* "Forget it, I'm leaving."

"Don't you want what you came for?" Cooper called after him. Luke turned around. Cooper's grin took up far too much of his face.

"I didn't come for anything."

"Sure you did."

"No. I didn't," Luke said angrily. "You think everyone who talks to you wants drugs?"

"Who said anything about drugs?" Cooper said, clearly trying to look appalled. He couldn't keep a straight face. "Hey," he said, laughing obnoxiously, "you don't have to feel bad about it. Really. And, dude, believe me, you look like you need it."

"I said I didn't want anything."

"Sure you don't," Cooper said patronizingly. "But, hey, let me know when that changes. I can get whatever. Ask anyone. Ask Applegate."

Luke froze. "What's that supposed to mean?" he demanded.

Cooper shrugged. "You know what I mean."

"What, you sell him pot?" It was no secret that Hayden smoked a little weed sometimes.

"Well, he needed a little more help than that." Cooper smirked. "He needs help a lot, really. It's sort of sad."

Luke shook his head. "You're high."

"Am I?" Cooper asked. "All right."

"Hayden doesn't . . . Hayden doesn't do that much." Luke rubbed his hand along the back of his neck.

"Okay," Cooper acquiesced. "My bad."

Luke glared at him. "I don't have time for this." He left, slamming Cooper's door behind him. He stomped back up to his room and, as he walked inside, kicked over the wastebasket by the door. It was empty. He took a breath, righted it, and sat down heavily on his bed. Cooper was a liar. Hayden would never do any of that crap. He was an athlete. He was way too smart for that.

A few nights later, Hayden returned. Luke was sitting on his bed, filling out some college applications to schools he didn't care at all about, when Hayden walked in.

"Hey."

"Hey."

Hayden set down his suitcase. He looked at the applications. "Oh." He crossed the room to look over Luke's shoulders. "So, uh, you get deferred?"

"Nope. Rejected." There was something sort of cathartic about saying it out loud.

"Huh." Hayden looked crushed. "Well, uh, you could always transfer later. You know, if you wanted. Like for sophomore year."

"Yep."

Hayden nodded slowly. "Yeah. You could transfer. Okay. Okay."

"Yeah." Luke watched his friend carefully. He didn't *seem* like he was still mad.

"So . . . how was your break?" Hayden asked.

Crap. "Okay. Yours?"

"Same."

They hesitated, staring at each other in awkward silence. Finally, Hayden burst out. "You know what, my break wasn't okay at all. It was really shitty."

Mine too, mine too, mine too. "Oh."

Hayden blushed crimson. He shifted from his right foot to his left. "Well, we're back, anyway."

"Yeah. Look, about before—"

"Forget it," Hayden broke in. "You weren't yourself." He looked to Luke for reassurance.

"Yeah," Luke said, and that was that.

CHAPTER 8

FENCING PRACTICES resumed at the end of the first week after winter break. The opening meet of the season was nearing, and the fencing gym was filled with tension and excitement. Luke arrived late, which was not unusual for him. He made a conscious effort not to worry about things like being on time. Too much anxiety over stuff like that wasn't good for him. Too much anxiety in general wasn't good. Luke didn't like what it could lead to.

The boys' team practiced on the right side of the gym, and the girls' team practiced on the left. Coach Dawson was walking back and forth across the gym to check on both teams. The boys' team had already divided up into squads based on the fencers' weapons of choice. The épée squad, led by Drew Devonshire and including Freddy Polk, was nearest to the door, doing drills while wearing heavy cloth sleeves to protect their arms. In the middle of the gym, the foil squad, led by an obnoxious senior named Ward McAfee, had divided into partners, who were taking turns chasing each other back and forth with their swords. In the back of the gym, Luke's own squad, the sabre squad, was setting up a machine.

The machine consisted of a small electric scoreboard with a red light and a green light and cords that connected to two reels positioned on either end of the fencing strip. When two fencers got onto the strip, they would each plug their body cords into a reel so that when one's sword connected with the other's metal jacket or mask, the red or green light would go off.

When Luke reached the back of the gym, the two sabre alternates were taping the reels to the floor so that they wouldn't slide down the strip. The alternates, Ben Sajjadi and Alex Dimenstein, were sophomores and inexperienced, but during a meet, if Briar was winning, sometimes Hayden would substitute one of them in for a tired starter. Hayden was the first sabre and squad leader, as well as a team captain. He was standing off to one side talking to Tristan Morris, the third sabre. Tristan, though a senior, was new to the varsity team this year, but he'd been doing pretty well. Tristan was tall and a little gawky, with curly brown hair and two prominent front teeth. He was a calm, pleasant sort of person, who always seemed sure of himself without being cocky.

Luke approached them sheepishly, feeling a little guilty about being late, and noticed a third person standing with Hayden and Tristan. Russell, dressed in an electric jacket and mask, leaned casually against the wall, gazing over their heads around the room. He saw Luke and gave him a little nod. Luke shot a questioning look at Hayden.

"We're doing king of the hill," said Hayden, walking toward him. "Everyone's in. Dawson wants to test out our new teammate." He said the last two words with such false gusto that Luke had to laugh. "So suit up," said Hayden. "We're about to start."

In king of the hill, one always started with the weakest fencers and moved up to the stronger ones, so that the former could get a couple of bouts in before being knocked out. As an insult, Hayden had them start off with Russell against Ben, the weakest alternate. Luke watched, curious, while putting on his electric gear. After the first few touches, Luke's curiosity turned to concern. Russell was good, seriously good. His footwork was perfect, he didn't lean too far forward, and he never missed a parry. He destroyed Ben quickly, 5–0. He then shook hands with Ben, waited while Alex plugged in to the machine, and proceeded to beat him, 5–0, as well. Coach Dawson walked past during the bout and said "yes, yes" a few times. Hayden, refereeing the bout, looked purple.

As Tristan walked onto the strip, Alex took over refereeing. Luke moved next to Hayden. "He's good," he whispered.

Hayden shrugged, trying to appear nonchalant. "He'll tire out." Luke wasn't so sure.

Tristan scored the first touch with a feint cut. Hayden cheered loudly, visibly relaxing. But Russell scored the next two with a jump back and a lightning-fast parry-riposte. "Morris!" Hayden shouted. "What the fuck are you doing? Wake up!"

Luke frowned. It wasn't like Hayden to yell at a teammate like that. "New guy's fast," he said in Tristan's defense.

Hayden snorted. "Please." They watched as Russell pushed Tristan back until he was off the strip. "Come on, Morris! Aggression!" It was no use. Russell defeated Tristan, 5–1.

"Next!" Russell called mockingly, laughing as he pulled his mask off to push the hair from his sweaty face.

Uh-oh, thought Luke. *Next would be me.*

"Do me a favor, Luke," said Hayden. "Beat the crap out of him."

Luke laughed weakly. "Yeah." He stepped nervously onto the strip and, after Tristan helped him plug in, trotted over to the starting mark and crouched into his en garde position.

"Ready," said Hayden, refereeing again. "Fence!"

Luke sprang forward and Russell did the same. They each got in two advances before they were in range of each other. Both lunged and both attacks hit. Both lights went off. "Simultaneous," declared Hayden.

Luke turned to gape at Hayden. Russell had lunged before him. It had been so clear. Russell's arm had been halfway out before Luke had even begun his attack. It should have been Russell's point. Hayden stared back at him, his face unreadable. Luke turned back to Russell, who was looking angry but saying nothing. *He won't argue because he won't give Hayden the opportunity to overrule him,* Luke realized. *I should argue for him.*

But he didn't. Instead, he stepped back and got en garde again. Through the black wire of his and Russell's masks, he could see Russell's eyes narrow. "En garde," said Hayden, jeeringly, to Russell, who did so silently.

"Ready . . . fence!" This time Russell parried Luke's attack smoothly, and only his light went off. Hayden had to give him the touch.

"Ready . . . fence!" Russell caught Luke under the guard while advancing.

"Ready . . . fence!" Luke's arm swung wide and Russell got him on his side.

"Ready . . . fence!" Russell beat Luke's blade to the side and whacked him across the shoulder.

"Ready . . . fence!" Luke parried, but then missed the riposte. He cringed as he felt Russell's sword tap him smartly on the head. "Bout."

Hayden was glowering at Luke when he stepped off the strip. "He's good," Luke offered feebly, but Hayden was already striding forward to fence Russell. Luke moved up to ref, but Hayden called meanly over his shoulder, "No, Morris, you do it. Give Prescott a minute to remember what sport this is."

Luke's face flushed, and he retreated as Tristan came forward with an apologetic smile in Luke's direction. *Not fair. Tristan barely did better than I did.* Hayden and Russell took their places on the strip, facing each other. Luke had a sinking feeling in his stomach. This could not go well. "Ready," said Tristan. "Fence!" Hayden and Russell charged forward, lunging out with their swords. Both lights went off, and there was a loud CRACK! Luke looked up in alarm as a piece of metal arched up into the air and landed a few feet away. It was the end of Hayden's sword. He had hit Russell's shoulder so hard that the blade had snapped in two.

Russell staggered back holding his shoulder in pain, and Hayden smirked. "You okay?" he asked, making it obvious he couldn't care less.

"Fine," Russell said curtly. He turned to Tristan. "Whose touch was that?"

Tristan looked at Luke. Luke shrugged. "I don't know," said Tristan. "I'm throwing it out."

"Fine," said Russell again. "Let's go," he told Hayden, and got back en garde.

Something slightly darker than amusement crossed Hayden's face. "All right," he said, tossing his broken sword to the side and picking up a new one. "Let's."

"Ready . . . fence!" Hayden took a few steps forward, then switched directions, forcing Russell to follow him down the end of the strip. Russell lunged, and Hayden flew backwards. The tip of Russell's blade missed Hayden's face by an inch, and Hayden lunged forward. Russell barely had time to pull the blade back to stop Hayden's sword from crashing down on his head. He made the parry clumsily, then lurched forward and slashed Hayden powerfully across the side. There was a hollow noise as the metal blade bashed against Hayden's ribs. Tristan called the touch to Russell, and Hayden limped back into en garde, trying unsuccessfully to look as if Russell's cut had barely hurt.

And so it went, back and forth. Both fencers seemed to care less about the score than inflicting pain on each other. At one point Hayden hit Russell so hard that Luke was sure he'd dislocated his shoulder. The next touch, Russell's blade "slipped" below the target area to hit Hayden between the legs. After each touch, Hayden and Russell returned fiercely to en garde, each one determined not to show any discomfort. Finally, the score was 4–4. The next point would win. "Ready . . . fence!" said Tristan, and Russell flew forward. Hayden made as if to move too, then stood perfectly still as Russell came at him. At the last minute, he jammed the thick, metal hilt of his sword into Russell's face.

Russell yelled loudly and twisted sideways. His mask flew off with the power of Hayden's punch. Luke had seen hilts collide with masks from time to time, but never with such deliberate force.

Across the gym, fencers turned to stare. Russell sank down, holding the side of his face, which was already turning red. "What happened?" cried Coach Dawson, rushing over from the girls' épée squad. "What happened?"

"He punched me!" Russell's voice was muffled by the hand clutching his jaw.

"It was an accident," said Hayden smoothly, the look of angry intensity gone from his face when he pulled off his mask. "Russ, man, are you okay?"

"He did it on purpose!" accused Russell.

Coach Dawson looked appalled. "Now," he started. "Now, the important thing is if you're all right."

Russell leapt to his feet. "He did it on purpose!" he repeated.

"It was an accident!" protested Hayden. "Luke, you saw it, right?"

Everyone turned to look at Luke. Luke stared down at his shoes. *That was no accident.* "Yeah," he said, hating himself. "Hayden didn't mean to."

Coach Dawson forced a smile. "There," he said, "now, let's not get angry." He put his hand on Russell's shoulder in a paternalistic sort of way. "We're a team here. You were doing so well before."

Sputtering, Russell looked back and forth between the smirking Hayden and the reddening Luke. He wheeled around to look at Tristan, Alex, and Ben. "You saw it," he said furiously. The three said nothing.

Coach Dawson seemed quite at a loss. "Come on, we'll go to the nurse. She'll fix you up and—"

"No," Russell interrupted coldly. "I want to finish the bout."

"You win," Hayden said with false earnestness. "That last touch was yours."

Coach Dawson glanced approvingly at Hayden. "Excellent, excellent."

Russell turned away. "I'm going to get a drink," he muttered, and stormed off.

The coach, flustered, headed back toward the épée squad, and Luke's squad was silent for a moment. "Well," Hayden said almost cheerfully. "Got rid of that idiot. For now, anyway." The sophomores laughed, eager to please their squad leader. Luke looked at Tristan, who gave him a none-of-our-business sort of shrug.

"Luke," said Hayden, grinning broadly to let him know he was back in his good graces. "Want to fence?"

Luke swallowed. "Yeah," he said, returning Hayden's smile. "Now that that asshole's gone."

CHAPTER 9

A FEW DAYS LATER, Luke cut math with Hayden and Freddy Polk, and the three went for a ride in Hayden's car, a silver Jaguar his parents had bought him for Christmas. Hayden hadn't said a word about the incident at practice, and Luke was happy not to talk about it. Hayden seemed a little embarrassed about the whole thing.

As they drove along the winding back roads of Forest County, Luke relaxed against the leather of the passenger seat and enjoyed the beautiful day. A song he didn't know was blaring out of the radio. He grinned. Things were okay. "Dude, I love this car," came Freddy's voice from the back seat. "I *love* this car."

Hayden beamed. "Check this out." He turned onto Kennelly Road, which was relatively straight. Luke heard the growl of the car picking up speed. He glanced over. The speedometer was climbing—sixty, seventy, eighty, ninety. It hit a hundred and held steady.

The road ended, and with a squeal of tires, Hayden turned sharply onto the next street. Luke laughed. "Psycho."

"Psycho, huh?" Slowing down only slightly, Hayden stuck his left arm out his window and his right arm out the sunroof, clasping them together on top of the car. He brought a knee up to guide the wheel.

"Hayden, we're going"—Luke checked—"eighty miles an hour."

"And now we're going ninety," said Hayden as the car sped up.

Freddy leaned over between the seats. "Hey, I bet you can't make that turn up there."

"Freddy—" Luke started. *Am I still having fun?*

"Twenty bucks says I can," said Hayden.

"Thirty," said Freddy.

Hayden laughed. "Thirty."

They reached the turn in the road, and Hayden leaned hard to the right, twisting his knees against the wheel. Luke sucked in his breath. A mailbox whizzed by his window missing him by inches, and finally they were pointed straight again. Luke had already let out his breath, had already starting laughing along with Hayden and Freddy when he saw the boy on the bicycle.

The boy was coming out of the driveway of one of the houses and obviously hadn't seen the car fly around the corner. Freddy yelled. Hayden froze. Luke lunged forward and grabbed the wheel, lurching it to the left. The car swerved, narrowly missing the bicycle and flying forward. Hayden slammed his foot on the brakes, and all three of them jerked in their seats.

"Shit," said Freddy.

"Shit," Hayden echoed.

Freddy leaned back in his seat. "That was . . ."

"Yeah." Hayden looked at Luke. "Good, uh . . . good looking out." He laughed nervously. "That was almost really bad."

"Um, yeah," Luke mumbled. "Let's slow it down a little."

"I need gas," Hayden said abruptly. He started the car again, his knuckles white on the steering wheel.

Luke wanted him to stop the car; he didn't want to ride anymore. But he said nothing, and the three of them drove on slowly and in silence. When they reached a main road, they pulled into the nearest gas station and Hayden got out.

There was an ice cream shop across the street from the gas station, and while Hayden filled up the tank, Luke and Freddy ran over to get cones and, as Hayden so eloquently put it, "to calm the fuck down a little."

The shop was almost empty except for a middle-aged man sitting by himself at a table and a teenage couple in a booth in the back. The man at the corner table had jowls and a thick mustache that was caked in mint ice cream. The couple had their backs to Luke, so he couldn't make out their faces. The boy's arm was draped around the girl's shoulder. Something about him gave Luke a weird feeling, like he'd seen him before. Something about the hair . . . all that blond hair . . . Just then the couple stood up to leave, and Luke got a look at their faces. Russell and Nicole.

Luke elbowed Freddy, who was staring obliviously up at the board of ice cream flavors. "Is that . . . ?"

Freddy looked. "Yeah."

"That is not good." Luke's stomach lurched as he watched Russell help Nicole put on her coat. They didn't seem to notice Luke or Freddy.

"Not at all," Freddy agreed. He paused. "Well. I mean, she and Hayden *are* broken up. So maybe it doesn't really matter?" Luke stared at him. Freddy winced. "Hayden's gonna flip."

"Uh-huh."

But as they told the story back in the car, Hayden's face remained scarily impassive. "So they're together now," he said.

"I-I don't know," Freddy stuttered. He looked at Luke, then back at Hayden. "Maybe. I guess."

"I knew there was something. Didn't I tell you?" Hayden said, turning to Luke and raking his left hand through his dark hair.

"Yeah," Luke said cautiously. "So I guess that's that."

Hayden nodded. "Well, it was over a long time ago."

Like weeks ago. "Yeah."

"Fuck them."

"Yeah."

CHAPTER 10

AFTER HAYDEN FOUND OUT about Russell and Nicole, Luke kept waiting for something to happen, for Hayden to snap. But he was remarkably civil. The news about the new couple spread around school, and Russell started to get even smugger, giving Hayden a big grin whenever they saw each other. Still, Hayden did nothing. In fact, he seemed oddly unaffected by the whole situation. Luke didn't trust it, but since Hayden didn't really want to talk to him about how he was feeling, Luke let the issue drop.

At fencing practices, however, Hayden's dislike for Russell was still very clear. He went out of the way to criticize him during drills and footwork, and sometimes he wouldn't let him fence electric with everyone else. Since Hayden was the squad leader, there wasn't much Russell could do about it other than complain to Coach Dawson, and the coach was already unimpressed with Russell after his "outburst" during his first practice.

"You don't think Dawson'll start him, do you?" Luke asked Hayden during practice one afternoon as Russell performed flawless draw cuts on a practice dummy.

"Not a chance," Hayden scoffed, slashing his own dummy aggressively.

"I don't know . . ." Luke said, admiring Russell's technique. "He's kind of . . ."

"What?" Hayden demanded.

Kind of good. "I don't know." Luke turned back to his dummy. He was also trying to do a draw cut, but the point of his blade kept getting stuck.

"There's just no way," Hayden said. "He just doesn't have it, you know what I mean?"

Not a clue. "Yeah."

"Dawson gets that. He and I have talked about it, actually."

Luke stopped practicing. "You went to Dawson?"

"Of course I did," Hayden said casually. "You don't want him starting, do you? I just explained to Dawson that he's not, you know, a team player. No sportsmanship. And it'd go better for us this season if it was just you and me and Morris. We'd be more comfortable that way. We'd fence better. And Dawson, you know, he was pretty agreeable." He grinned at Luke. "See? I take care of everything."

Luke frowned. Something didn't sound quite right about that. Before he could say anything, there was a loud clatter. They turned. Tristan had dropped his sabre. "Sorry," he said cheerily as he retrieved it. "My bad."

Hayden groaned. "Why is this squad so tragic?"

Luke shrugged. *We're not that bad.*

"Morris!" Hayden called out. "Maybe next time you could try to hang on to the sword?"

"You got it!" Tristan called back.

Hayden turned back to Luke. "You got it!" he mimicked, affecting Tristan's goofy grin. Luke laughed, even though he wasn't sure if it was funny.

"That guy," Hayden said, "is so annoying."

"Why?"

Hayden rolled his eyes. "I don't know. He's just so fucking smiley all the time. It's weird."

"Guess so . . ."

"Anyway, like I was saying, I'm taking care of it. There's just no way Conrad's gonna be varsity on my team. And who knows? Maybe if he can't compete, he'll quit."

"You really think he'd quit?" Luke asked. "He seems pretty into it."

They watched him attack the dummy with excellent technique. Hayden frowned. "He'll quit. Eventually, he'll quit."

Russell suddenly caught sight of Luke and Hayden standing there, staring at him. He probably knew they were talking about him. Instead of looking embarrassed or angry, he sent them a mocking little wave. Hayden gave Luke a look of disgust, and they both turned away.

"Hey, Applegate!" Russell called.

Hayden's voice was calm. "What." It wasn't a question.

"You read a lot of magazines, Applegate?" Russell asked, sauntering over. "Sometimes you can read the most *interesting* stuff in magazines."

Hayden glared at him. "Do I look like I give a fuck?"

"Actually, I found something today that you might be interested in," Russell drawled. "Maybe I'll show you."

"I don't even care what you're talking about," Hayden said. "Get back to work."

Luke glanced down at his watch. "We're done, actually."

"Okay," Hayden said, still looking at Russell. "Then just get away from me." Russell smirked, but he walked away.

I don't think I want to know what that was about.

The team put away their equipment and headed toward the locker room. Luke hung back to practice his draw cut a little more. Russell's perfect one had made him a little self-conscious. He only practiced for a few minutes because his legs were pretty sore. With just two weeks before the first meet of the season, training had intensified. Heavy footwork and drilling were now accompanied by a series of plyometric exercises that left Luke's legs aching. When he finally staggered out of the gym, he nearly collided with a couple of people who were standing just outside the door. "Oops, sorry," he said, and then froze. It was Tristan and Rachel Howard, the purple-haired junior from Luke's Spanish class.

She smiled vaguely at him. "No problem."

Say something cool. "Tired," he pointed out astutely. Rachel just stared at him.

"Me too," Tristan rescued him. "My legs feel totally dead."

"So, what's going on with you guys?" Luke asked, and then was instantly aware of how awkward he sounded.

"Actually, we were just talking about the Phi Ep party this weekend," said Tristan. "Are you going?"

Luke hadn't given it that much thought. "Yeah. Definitely. Can't wait." Briar students regularly crashed the local frat parties at Forest College; no one seemed to mind, though occasionally some drunk brother would make a show of kicking them out.

"You can come with us if you want," offered Rachel.

She's asking me out. She's totally asking me out.

No, she's not. She said come with us. She's going with Tristan, too. It's not a date. Chill out.

"I want." He laughed. "I mean, yeah."

"Okay, cool," she said.

"I'm gonna go change," Luke said. "I'll catch you guys later." He started for the locker room, then turned around. "Is it okay if Hayden comes, too?"

"Sure," Rachel said with a grin. "Bring your boyfriend."

He rolled his eyes at her, called back "thanks," and entered the locker room feeling like an idiot. The sight that greeted him made him forget all about Rachel Howard out in the hallway.

Hayden was standing on one of the low benches, pushing Russell's head against a wall of lockers. His face was red, and his eyes were bulging. His mouth was twisted into a wide howl, and he was screaming, "You son of a bitch, you little fuck! I'll kill you!"

"Hayden, let him go! Let him go!" Drew Devonshire was standing behind Hayden, his arms wrapped around Hayden's torso, trying unsuccessfully to pull him away from Russell.

Hayden wasn't listening. He pulled Russell's head back and then slammed it viciously back down against the lockers. "I will *end* you, do you hear me? I will fucking *kill* you!"

Luke lurched forward. He rushed between the bench and the lockers and planted a hand on Hayden's chest, pushing hard. Hayden lost his balance and fell backwards into Drew. Russell collapsed, gasping, to the ground. Hayden was fighting against Drew, who was trying desperately to restrain him.

"Let me go!" Hayden was shouting. "I'll tear his fucking head off! Let me go!"

"Hayden, stop!" Luke cried, horrified. He'd never seen Hayden this out of control. Hayden struggled for a moment more, but Drew had both of his arms pinned firmly behind his back. Then, abruptly, he went limp, panting and staring straight at Russell. "What happened?" Luke demanded, looking first at Hayden, then at Drew. Neither of them answered. He turned around to Russell, who was getting to his feet. A large bruise was already beginning to form on the side of his forehead. "What happened?" Luke repeated.

Drew tentatively relaxed his hold on Hayden, who shrugged away from him. To Luke's relief, he didn't lunge at Russell. He just leaned back against the opposite wall of lockers, still staring at the floor. Then Russell started laughing. It was a low laugh, a little throaty, since Russell was out of breath. It came in short jerks, like the pull of a saw across firewood. Luke turned on Russell. "What the hell?"

"Jesus," said Russell in between laughs. He looked at Hayden. "Can't take a joke, can you?"

"Get out of here," Drew hissed. Hayden said nothing.

Russell cracked his neck and pushed past Luke. He turned back, still laughing a little. "No sense of humor? Seriously, Applegate?"

"Out!" roared Drew, and with a smirk and a toss of blond hair, Russell was gone.

"What happened?" Luke asked for what felt like the hundredth time. "What joke?"

Drew looked at Hayden, then back at Luke. "Russell, he . . . he had a—"

Hayden smacked his own head back against the lockers. The metallic crash echoed through the room. He pulled away from the lockers and glared at Luke and Drew. "Fuck you both," he said, and left.

"Okay, seriously, *what?*" Luke demanded. He thought he at least had a right to know why he'd just been insulted.

"Russell Conrad is a waste of skin," Drew declared.

"What did he do?"

"I guess it was in a tabloid or something. I mean, that's what you get when your dad works in Hollywood."

"What about Hayden's dad?" Luke asked. Philip Applegate was a semi-famous movie director. Last summer, when Luke had gone to visit Hayden in Los Angeles, Mr. Applegate had given them a tour of the set of his newest film.

"It was bullshit, probably. Probably wasn't even true. But Russell had this clipping, and he showed it to Hayden. Waved it in his face."

"What did it say?" Luke asked, now purely out of curiosity.

Drew reddened. "It's none of my business," he said pointedly. "I mean, I just don't think it's something Hayden would want his friends talking about." He shrugged. "Ask him yourself."

"Yeah, I don't think so," Luke said, smiling nervously. "I've got a feeling he might be kind of touchy about it."

CHAPTER 11

LUKE DIDN'T SAY a word to Hayden when he got back to the dorm, and Hayden ignored him completely for the rest of the day. He just paced around the room, occasionally offering a kick at an unsuspecting wastebasket or chair leg. It was a very tense evening.

But in the morning, Hayden was as cheerful as ever. He woke Luke up for breakfast with the usual pillow to the head and chatted brightly as they headed down to the dining hall. Luke was so thrown by his best friend's sudden change of attitude that he said nothing about yesterday afternoon's excitement. He didn't want to ever see Hayden that angry again.

As they were waiting in line to get their trays, Luke mentioned the Phi Ep party he'd agreed to go to with Tristan and Rachel.

"I thought we were going to go with Freddy and Drew and Courtney," said Hayden, though Luke couldn't remember such a plan ever being discussed.

"Oh, yeah, I mean, we could," Luke stammered. "It's just I told Rachel we'd go with her. Her and Tristan, I mean. They invited me. Us. So I didn't want to be rude or whatever."

A slow smile spread across Hayden's face. "Rachel's that girl with the hair, right?"

"Yeah," said Luke, a little too defensively.

Hayden's smile widened. "Why, Lucas, have we a crush?"

"Shut up."

"Luke and Rachel," Hayden stated experimentally. "Has a nice ring to it, don't you think?"

"Go to hell," Luke shot back. *It does have a rather nice ring to it, though.*

"So are you going to ask her to be your girlfriend?" Hayden teased. "Going to take her to the prom?"

"You really suck, you know that?" Luke hissed, twisting around to make sure that no one was overhearing the conversation.

Hayden chuckled. "All right, all right, sorry." He took a deep breath. "Luke Prescott, in the interest of romance—namely, yours—I shall accept an inferior ride to this party . . . so that you can get with the girl with the hair."

"You're such a martyr."

"This is true."

On Saturday night, Luke and Hayden met up with Rachel and Tristan in the school's parking lot, where they climbed into Rachel's old and decrepit station wagon to drive to Forest College. When they arrived, the Phi Epsilon fraternity house was teeming with people. The air was hot and thick, and the music was deafening. Everyone was dancing.

"This is insane!" Hayden shouted over the noise.

"This is awesome!" Tristan yelled.

This is ridiculous, Luke thought.

Luke quickly found himself lost in the crowd of people. His sneakers kept sticking to the disgusting floor. He looked for Rachel, but she had disappeared. The music was so loud and everyone was moving so fast. He didn't see anyone he knew. He wanted to leave.

Someone put their hand on Luke's shoulder, and he turned around. Rachel was standing there, smiling at him from underneath her choppy purple bangs. She looked pretty. Luke beamed. "Hey."

"Crazy, isn't it?" Rachel said, gesturing around at the party.

Luke nodded. "Uh-huh." *Clever, Luke.*

"Do you want to dance?" she asked him.

"Uh, yeah. Yes. Yeah." He could feel himself blush, but Rachel just laughed and led him out into the crowd of people.

Luke had always been a terrible dancer. He never knew what to do with his arms or his legs, and he was always too self-conscious to move to the rhythm. But that night at the party, dancing with Rachel, Luke started to feel at ease. He started to feel confident. Carefree. Relaxed.

And of course, Rachel had to ruin it all and kiss him.

It was a quick kiss, slightly awkward and spontaneous. She just leaned up, tilting her head back, and put their lips together. It was over before Luke actually registered it in his mind. As she pulled away, she smiled at him. Luke smiled back goofily.

Say something.

Rachel started to look a little embarrassed.

Say something.

She stopped dancing.

Say something.

"Was it okay that I did that?" she asked him.

"Yeah! Yeah, I mean, yeah. It was, yeah. Way okay." *Way okay? What am I saying?*

Rachel laughed. "You just look a little shocked."

Luke was sure his face was flaming red. "A little. I mean, I'd thought maybe you and Tristan . . ."

"No. We're just friends," she answered.

"Cool."

"Yeah?"

"Yeah." And then it started to rain.

Some drunk guys on the second floor were dumping wastebaskets filled with water over the second-floor railing, and it poured down on the partygoers below. There were shrieks of terror or delight or both, and Luke and Rachel both rushed to safer ground. In the stampede they were separated, and Luke found himself on the stairs without Rachel. He looked around, but he couldn't see her. Maybe she'd made it to the second floor. He headed upstairs to look for her.

From the staircase, he spotted Drew and Courtney down below, leaning against a wall, their arms and legs locked around each other like puzzle pieces. It didn't seem like they wanted to be interrupted, so he continued climbing. He reached the second-floor landing and turned to see Hayden talking to someone whose face he couldn't see. He started to approach when the person shifted to his left and Luke got a good look. It was Cooper Albright.

Luke watched Hayden dig into his pocket and pull out a roll of cash as Cooper surreptitiously handed him a tiny plastic bag. Luke had seen enough. He felt sick. He had to get out of there.

He walked around the corner only to find himself face-to-face with Russell Conrad. "Hey, Luke!" Russell staggered forward, stumbled against the wall, and slid downward into a sitting position.

Nodding curtly, Luke started to walk away, but Russell reached out and grabbed at his leg, nearly tripping him. "Werr yuh guh-in?"

Luke noticed the beer bottle in the crook of Russell's arm. "Dude, you're trashed." Russell giggled. "How many of those have you had?"

"Furr . . . fife . . ." He shrugged.

"You got a ride home?" Luke asked, surprised at himself for caring.

"Yurr a good frennn, Luke," Russell slurred.

"Russell, do you have a ride home?" Luke repeated. *I am not your friend.*

"Yeh, yeh, yeh . . ." He stood, shakily, then tripped, spilling some of his beer onto the front of Luke's shirt.

"Oh, man!" Luke backed away, disgusted. Russell looked crestfallen. Luke sighed. "You're not driving?" he clarified.

"Naw," said Russell. Reassured, Luke twisted away and continued down the hall. He entertained briefly the idea of offering Russell a ride home with him and his friends, but he knew that it would make Hayden furious.

Luke tried for a few more minutes to find Rachel, but the frat house was too crowded. He just had to hope they ran into each other. He spent the next hour or so meandering through the party, occasionally running into people he knew and trying to forget about what he'd just seen Hayden doing. Maybe it was a mistake. Maybe

Hayden wasn't buying drugs. Or maybe the drugs weren't for him—maybe they were for a friend. This could all be one huge misunderstanding.

Finally, around midnight, Luke went off in search of a non-intoxicated ride home. He managed to locate a very buzzed Tristan by the top of the stairs, and, a few minutes later, he spotted Hayden helping a tipsy Rachel into the front hall and coaxing the keys out of her hand. Hayden took one look at Luke and said, "Looks like I'm driving home tonight." Luke glanced down at himself and realized he had beer all over his shirt. He didn't feel like explaining. Not to Hayden and not tonight.

"That'd probably be a good idea," Tristan mumbled, leaning heavily against Luke's shoulder.

An image of Cooper handing Hayden the little plastic bag flashed through Luke's mind, but he brushed it away while Tristan managed to get Rachel into the back seat, then out while she threw up, then back in. Hayden got into the driver's seat, Luke got into the back with Rachel, and Tristan climbed into the front. Hayden was joking and laughing, and talking a mile a minute about how great the party had been. He seemed fine. A little hyper, but fine. It would all be okay. By the time Hayden was turning the keys in the ignition, Luke had himself so convinced that he barely noticed the slight tremor in Hayden's hands.

Luke never lost consciousness. Not when the car spun off the road. Not when Hayden shoved his foot again and again on the unresponsive brakes. Not when the car hit the tree. Not when Luke and Rachel smashed up against their seat belts. Not when Tristan flew through the windshield.

CHAPTER 12

LUKE WAS STUCK, wedged between the seat and the smashed-up front of the car. He thought he might be able to extricate himself from his painful position, but he was scared of making things worse. His back was twisted, and he could feel a sharp pain in his forehead where he'd hit the seat in front of him. He couldn't see Tristan, but he'd watched him go through the windshield and he knew that couldn't be good.

Okay, he told himself, *this is the part where you hear the sirens. And the police and paramedics come and they put you on a gurney and you go to the . . . clean place.* He couldn't think of the word for it and it terrified him. What if he was permanently brain-damaged?

He heard a groan next to him, and he made the gamble of turning his head. Rachel was shoving open the door on her side, and, thankfully, it fell open. Luke saw her stagger out. She was standing. *Good, that's good, that's really good.*

Rachel came around the other side of the car. Luke couldn't see her anymore because he was too afraid to turn his head all the way around. His head was pounding and his neck felt like it might snap if he twisted it. He heard the door open and felt Rachel's tiny hands on his shoulders, dragging him out of the car. His torso caught on the seat belt, and the wind was knocked out of him. Rachel swore and reached over to unbuckle the seat belt. Moments later Luke was lying on the grass, where he could see just how far they were from the road.

"Luke, hey, talk to me," she was saying.

"Am I okay?" he asked. It was a stupid thing to say, as if Rachel would know. But he wanted to make sure he had all his limbs, and Rachel seemed like she was in a better position to tell.

"You're going to be okay, Luke, don't worry."

Luke stood shakily and checked himself over. He touched his hand against his forehead and was instantly sorry. His hand came away with blood. Rachel was staring at him, her green eyes wide and worried. She didn't look banged up at all, but she was shaking in a way that made Luke think she wasn't really aware of it.

Other than the cut on his head, Luke started to think he was all right, and he and Rachel walked around to the front of the car to check on Hayden and Tristan. Hayden was slumped against the steering wheel, unconscious. Tristan was out cold, lying on the hood of the car. His head was a few inches from the trunk of the tree that the car was wrapped around. Luke wasn't sure whether or not Tristan had hit his head on the tree.

There was blood everywhere, and it took Luke a few seconds to see why. Tristan's body was on the hood of the car, but his leg was hooked on the dashboard, and the glass from the windshield was cutting into his calf. Rachel doubled over and vomited for the second time that night. Luke felt like doing the same.

"Should we move him?" Luke asked nervously. The blood from his forehead was wet and sticky down the left side of his face.

"We have to call someone. Do you have your cell?"

"I think so." Luke reached into his pocket and pulled out the cell phone. Reception. *Thank God.*

It took a few minutes for the ambulance to come. The siren was blaring, and Luke's head hurt so badly he had to lean against the car. He let his surroundings fade to a blur as the paramedics rushed around and ushered him into an ambulance that brought him to the hospital. He had a cut on his head that needed a few stitches, but he was all right. The hard part came when they asked whom they should call for him. He debated momentarily as to whether to ask them to call his mother. He decided not to.

He was discharged quickly and found Rachel in the waiting room. She was crumpled sideways into a stiff wooden chair, her legs sticking out over one armrest, her head resting on the other. When she saw him coming, she sat up, swinging her legs forward and casting him a small smile. Rachel had talked her parents into not coming all the way from Connecticut, considering the fact that she was virtually unharmed. Rachel told Luke that Tristan was in the OR, getting surgery on his leg. Luckily, his head had missed the tree.

"Are you going to be okay?" he asked, sitting down next to her.

She rested her head on his shoulder. "Yeah. I'm just tired."

"Me too."

"That . . ."

"Yeah."

"My friend Rebecca's coming to pick me up," she told him. "She could drive you back to Briar, too."

"Thanks, yeah, that'd be good."

"No problem."

"Have you seen Hayden?" he asked her.

"Yeah, I went in to see him while you were getting stitches. He's okay; he's got a mild concussion. But he has to spend the night in the hospital."

"Oh. I think I'm gonna go see him." Luke stood. Then he turned back to Rachel. "Is that okay?" *Is it okay to leave you?*

"Yeah. Go ahead. I'm not going anywhere," she mumbled, snuggling back into the chair, her eyes drifting shut. She was still a little drunk.

When Luke finally managed to locate Hayden's room, Hayden was lying on the bed in a hospital gown. His eyes were closed and he wasn't moving. He looked asleep, but Luke couldn't tell. A machine in the back of the room was bleeping steadily. *Steady. Steady is good.*

Hayden looked so different, lying in the hospital bed. He looked younger, smaller. His hair was matted around his face, and a dark bruise had formed across the left side of his forehead. He looked damaged. "Hayden?"

After a moment Hayden's eyes flicked open, and his face broadened into his usual lopsided grin. "Luke!" And things started to be okay.

"How are you feeling?"

Hayden shrugged. "I'm all right. No worries."

"Good," Luke said, sitting down uneasily on the chair next to the bed. It was plastic and uncomfortable.

"Man, that was nuts, huh?" Hayden said nervously.

"Yeah."

"They did like a Breathalyzer. Good thing I wasn't drinking."

"Yeah, me either," said Luke.

"Really? 'Cause your shirt . . ."

"Some guy spilled it on me," Luke said, making a vague cup-in-hand gesture. He didn't bother to tell Hayden it was Russell. He didn't want to upset him.

"Oh," Hayden said.

"Tristan and Rachel had a few, I think."

"They okay?"

"Rachel's fine. She's outside. Tristan's still in surgery. Messed up his leg pretty bad."

"That sucks," Hayden said, leaning back once again and closing his eyes for a second.

"Hey . . . Hayden?"

Eyes open. "Yeah?"

"Did they do a tox screen on you?"

"A what?"

"A tox screen, like for drugs."

Hayden blinked. "No. You?"

"No, they didn't. I was just asking because . . ."

"What?"

Luke sighed. "I kind of saw you with Cooper at the party."

Hayden was quiet for a while. "Oh."

"Yeah."

Hayden took a deep breath and sat up straight. "Okay. Yeah. I got some stuff from Cooper, but I didn't even take it yet."

Luke cleared his throat. "What was it?"

Hayden's eyes wandered. "Coke."

"Coke? Seriously?"

"I just needed . . . I don't know. It was stupid. Whatever. Just stupid shit. I didn't even take it."

"Oh," said Luke. "So where is it?"

"What?"

"Where's the stuff you got from Cooper?"

Hayden stiffened. "What do you mean?"

"Well, the cops didn't find it at the scene. And the hospital didn't get hold of it, meaning it wasn't on you. So . . . if you didn't take it at the party, what happened to it?"

Hayden's face flamed. "Uh . . ."

"Oh, Hayden." *How could you?*

"She's pregnant!" Hayden said abruptly.

"Who? Nicole?"

"No! Mindy!"

"Oh!" Luke waited for this to sink in. *Hang on.* "Who the hell is Mindy?"

"That bitch my dad's been seeing," Hayden said coldly.

"I didn't know your parents were separated."

"They're not," said Hayden.

"Oh." *Oh.* Luke suddenly understood what that tabloid clipping must have been about.

"And he's all nice and *slick* and says he doesn't want our family to split up," Hayden spat out. "And he says he'll take care of the baby and that's it, that it's over with her." Hayden's head was back, as if he were talking to the ceiling. "And he was like, 'This is going to be your brother or sister.' And what the fuck? Like I'm going to play big brother to his bastard? No fucking way!"

"Well—" Luke started, but Hayden was venting and was not to be halted.

"I mean, it *was* over! And she just shows up *on Christmas Eve*, and she's all about how *sorry* she is that this happened!"

"Jesus, Hayden, I didn't know."

"Yeah," Hayden said through half-clenched teeth, suddenly looking more tired than Luke had ever thought possible.

"Listen, Hayden—"

Just then a nurse came in. "Visiting hours are over. Actually, they were over before you all got here. And he needs his rest," she said pointedly.

In an instant Hayden was back to his normal, nonchalant self. "Go on, I'm fine."

Luke stood. "Guess I'll see you in the morning?" It was meant to be a statement but came out as a question.

Hayden nodded. "Yeah."

"Bye."

He headed out the door and was stopped as he was leaving by a tremendously fat man in a police officer's uniform. *Uh-oh.* The man told Luke he had to ask him a few questions. He led him into an empty exam room and proceeded to grill him for at least twenty minutes. Luke didn't know what to say. He didn't mention the drugs; he didn't want Hayden to get into trouble. All he said was that the car had spun off the road and that the brakes had failed. The officer seemed to accept the story, because eventually he let Luke leave.

Luke doubted he had ever left a building as quickly as he walked out of the hospital with Rachel and her friend Rebecca. He had an overpowering urge to break out into a run, to get as far away as possible. Covering for Hayden when he skipped practice was one thing. Covering for Hayden when he crashed a car into a tree while on drugs? That was a little more complicated.

Luke couldn't calm down, not from the time he left the hospital until he went to bed that night. He felt like he ought to be doing—or feeling—something. Guilt, maybe? Over the years there had been various instances where Luke had felt the need to lie, but this lie, an omission of the truth to a police officer no less, this was Luke's first *official* lie.

Forget about it. It's over. Get some sleep. Hayden. The car crash. Drugs. Mindy. What kind of a name is Mindy? Forget about it. Go to sleep. Rachel. The hospital. Surgery. Blood. Sleep!

As he lay there in bed, Luke's mind inexplicably dragged him back to a trip his family had taken years ago. It was the summer he was fourteen. Jason had just gotten back from his first year at Briar, and their parents decided to visit Luke's grandparents. The drive had been fun. On the way back, they stopped at a hotel, one of those fancy places Luke's mother had always insisted they stay at. Everything in their rooms was meticulously prepared, right down to a folded corner on the edge of the toilet paper.

Luke remembered waking up in the middle of the night and seeing his father kneeling on the floor of the bathroom, folding and unfolding the corners of the paper. "Can't get it right, can't get it right," he was muttering over and over again. Luke had sat on his bed in horror, just watching. Finally, he stood up, went over, and pulled his father's hands away from the roll. His father had stared up at him, as if waking from a dream. His eyes had looked straight through him.

Luke had never told anyone about that night at the hotel, not his mother, not Jason, not Hayden. His father never mentioned it either.

CHAPTER 13

LUKE BORROWED the Jaguar and drove Hayden home from the hospital the next morning. They awkwardly avoided the subject of the night before, and Luke was sure Hayden was as relieved as he was when they finally got back to Briar.

Drew, Courtney, and Freddy were waiting for them in the parking lot with a hastily made sign on a sheet of lined paper. It read: WELCOME HOME, IDIOT! Beneath that someone had thoughtfully added in pencil: GLAD YOU DIDN'T DIE!

Hayden stepped out of the car with a flourish and a bow. In response, Freddy crumpled up the sign and threw it at him. There was plenty of laughter and talking as the group headed for the quad at the center of campus. They all teased Drew and Courtney about hooking up at the Phi Epsilon party, Hayden walked with his arm across Luke's shoulders, and Luke started to forget that anything was wrong. Then they ran into Nicole Johnston.

She was alone, which had become less unusual for her recently. She was wearing her backpack, obviously headed for the library, and she did a clumsy sort of double take when she saw them all coming toward her. The conversation abruptly stopped. "Hey," she said loudly. No one answered. Hayden smirked. Nicole rolled her eyes. "Are you really going to be such a toddler about this whole thing?" she asked him. Again, no one spoke. "Seriously, grow up." Her lips were pressed together in annoyance.

"Do you hear something?" Drew said quietly. He looked around and through Nicole. "Because I can't hear a thing."

"Oh, that's really mature." Nicole turned to Courtney. "Court, can you tell him he's an idiot?"

Nicole's best friend opened her mouth as Drew's arm snaked around her stomach. Courtney looked behind her at Hayden and Freddy and Luke. She looked back at Nicole. "Maybe you should go hang out with your new boyfriend."

Nicole recoiled, as if slapped. Luke felt like saying something, telling his friends they were being assholes, but Hayden's arm was around his shoulders, and he couldn't seem to make himself speak. So he let Nicole push past him, with her eyes suddenly lowered toward the ground, and he said nothing as they continued on to the quad.

"Ugh, I got so trashed last night," Drew said, picking up where the conversation had left off. "Guess you got a little buzzed, too, huh, Hayden?"

"Maybe . . ." said Hayden with a wink.

"So what happened?" Freddy asked. "Come on, gory details."

Hayden beamed, and Luke thought back to the first time he'd met his best friend. The first day of freshman orientation, he'd gone up to his new dorm room and seen Hayden there, unpacking. Luke had been so nervous, desperately wanting to be liked and to have at least one friend at this new school. Hayden had been all confidence. He'd asked if Luke wanted to go hang out at the Grill, a local restaurant, and Luke had said yes, and when they got there people had flocked around Hayden, laughing at his jokes and listening to his stories about growing up in Hollywood. The whole time, though, Hayden had stuck with Luke. Even when a group of his new friends invited him out with them that night, Hayden had insisted that Luke come, too. And it became very clear to Luke, very early on, that whatever Hayden wanted, Hayden got. So standing next to Hayden seemed like an attractive place to be.

At the moment, though, Luke was feeling a little uncomfortable. He didn't want to hear Hayden talk about the accident like it was some big, exciting story. They reached the quad, and Hayden flopped down on the grass. His friends followed suit. "It was crazy!" said Hayden, laughing. "Morris went through the fucking windshield!"

Stop laughing.

"I mean, he just went flying. And we were spinning around and it was nuts!" Hayden tossed back his head, a broad smile on his face.

Stop it.

"Were you scared?" Courtney asked, hanging on Hayden's every word.

Hayden shrugged. "I mean, it was freaky, yeah, but you know . . . it was actually kind of a rush!"

"Shut up." Luke barely recognized his own speaking voice.

Hayden turned in surprise. "Luke . . ."

"No, y-you don't get to do that. You don't get to p-pass it off like—" He was standing now, sputtering. "Tristan is in the *hospital*. He could have *died*. It's not a joke!"

Hayden stood, visibly alarmed. "Hey. Hey, I'm sorry." He placed a hand on Luke's shoulder. "You know me, I'm a moron. Come on."

Luke glanced around him. His friends were staring at him with looks of concern. He felt a rush of embarrassment. He knew his face was bright red. "Yeah. Yeah, no, *I'm* sorry." He shuffled his feet. "Guess I'm still a little wired. Whatever."

"No worries," said Hayden easily.

"I think I'm gonna go back to the dorm," Luke told him. "I'm tired." His friends didn't argue.

CHAPTER 14

THE NEXT WEEK flew by. News of the car crash spread around school, and Luke found himself constantly fielding questions from people he barely knew. Hayden loved the attention, but Luke despised it. No one seemed to realize how serious the accident had been, not even Hayden. Every time he heard Hayden telling the story of the crash, Luke had to fight to keep from yelling at him again. But he managed to keep his mouth shut, thankfully. His friends had thought he was weird enough the first time.

"I don't get it," Rachel said one afternoon when they were having lunch together in the dining hall. "Why do you care so much about what they'll think?" Rachel was the one person Luke was able to really talk to about the accident. They were both horrified by what had happened—and by what could have happened.

Luke shrugged. "This is high school. Everybody cares what everybody else thinks."

She laughed. "Point taken." She turned and glanced at Luke's friends, who were sitting a couple of tables away. The group was deep in conversation, but every now and then someone would look over at Luke and Rachel and laugh.

"I'll kill them later," Luke offered.

"That would be nice."

Luke smiled. He was starting to feel more comfortable with Rachel. Once he'd stopped mumbling like an idiot, he'd found that she was interesting to talk to. Not that he spent much time listening to her. Mainly he just watched the way her lips moved when she spoke. But she hadn't kissed him again yet, much to Luke's disappointment, and he was far from having the courage to initiate a kiss himself.

"Tristan's coming back to school tomorrow," she told him.

"Yeah? His leg's healed?"

"It's a lot better, I think," she answered. "And they put him on painkillers. He says he feels okay."

"You went to see him?" Luke asked.

"No, just over the phone."

"Oh." Luke wasn't sure if he liked the idea of Tristan and Rachel talking on the phone. He wondered if they did that a lot. He wondered who had called whom.

"A group of us are going to go over to bring him back from the hospital. You want to come?" she asked. "Maybe you could get some of the guys from the team to go?"

"Maybe," said Luke. He wished they weren't still talking about Tristan.

"I think he'd feel better if they came," she went on. "He already feels bad enough about being out for the beginning of the season."

Luke winced. That was a sore subject right now. Tristan wouldn't be in any shape to fence any time soon, and even once he came back, he'd be rusty. A replacement was needed, and the best JV fencer was Russell Conrad. Hayden had been less than thrilled, to say the least, but even he couldn't make the argument for starting one of the terrible sophomore alternates.

Rachel rolled her eyes as a loud peal of laughter erupted from Luke's friends' table. "Do they think they're being subtle?" she asked.

Luke pushed back his chair. "I'll go make them shut up."

"No, it's fine," she said, resting her hand on his forearm to stop him. "We'll just ignore them."

He grinned. Her hand was on his arm. "Okay."

Rachel laughed. "You're so . . ."

"What?"

"Transparent."

His face flushed. "I, um—"

"No, no," she said quickly. "It's not a bad thing. I like that I can kind of tell what you're thinking sometimes." She smiled. "Usually, I hate it when people are just trying so hard to be cool."

"I'm not—"

"Of course you are. But it's okay, because you're so hilariously obvious about it."

He didn't know whether he should be pleased or offended. He wasn't sure if he was being insulted or complimented. He decided he didn't care, because her hand was still there. "Well," he said truthfully, "I like that I never have any idea what you're thinking."

She giggled. "Okay. Good."

The bell rang, signaling the end of the lunch hour. Rachel headed off to class. Luke, who had a free period, ducked back to rejoin his friends. "You guys are such assholes," he groaned, as he slid into a seat at their table. Freddy and Courtney had gone to class, but Drew and Hayden were also free.

"Hey, we were just happy for you that you were actually able to *talk* to her this time," Hayden teased. "Instead of, you know, that weird mumbling thing you were doing."

"Yeah, that was weird," Drew said.

"I hate both of you." They laughed. "Actually," Luke remembered, "Rachel asked me something. Tristan's getting out of the hospital tomorrow, and some people are going to go pick him up. She wants to know if we want to go."

Drew looked blankly at him. "Why?"

"You know, to go and get him. Welcome him back or whatever."

"Won't his . . . friends want to do that?" Hayden asked.

"Oh." Luke's face reddened. "Yeah, well, I guess. But I mean, since we're his teammates . . ."

"Well, not right now, we aren't," Drew pointed out.

"Yeah," said Hayden. "He can't fence right now, can he?"

And whose fault is that? "Yeah, but—"

"Look, Luke," Hayden broke in. "If you want to go because you and Rachel are doing whatever you're doing, that's cool, obviously. But Drew and me, you know, we're busy then."

I didn't even tell you when they were going. "Yeah." Luke shrugged. "All right." There was a pause. Drew and Hayden were staring at him. "You know, actually . . . I think I'm busy then, too. Oh well."

Hayden nodded. "Cool."

CHAPTER 15

THE NEXT MONDAY there was a team meeting in the athletic center for all the varsity fencers. Russell was there, looking a little nervous and out of place. Luke was glad. He was glad that Russell didn't feel at ease. He shouldn't. He didn't belong there. He'd done nothing but mess things up since he'd gotten to Briar. *We'd all have been better off if he'd just stayed in Texas.*

In moments the meeting was under way, and Hayden's co-captain, Ward McAfee, immediately took control. His voice was monotonous, and Luke tuned him out until he got to talking about the meet coming up on Wednesday. He sent an eye roll toward Hayden, who looked just as bored as Luke felt.

"We should be in the gym by six," Ward was informing the team.

Luke groaned, already feeling the sleep deprivation that was bound to hit him on the morning of the meet.

"So if we leave in the morning, when's Russell gonna jump?" someone asked.

Suddenly, Hayden looked interested. "Yeah," he said slowly. "I mean, he's gotta jump. Otherwise, he can't fence."

"It's the rule," Luke put in out of loyalty to his friend.

"He can jump tomorrow," Ward said.

Russell nodded mildly. "Okay."

"Luke and I will take him," Hayden offered.

We will?

"Great," Russell said, sarcasm lining the word.

"Unless he's scared," Hayden said.

"Not a chance," Russell said flippantly, but his eyes started to narrow.

"I think he's scared," Hayden said to Luke, grinning maniacally.

"He says he'll jump, so we'll see," Luke said simply, to Hayden's disappointment. *I'm not anybody's crony.*

"Fine," Hayden said.

"Fine," Russell repeated.

This is such a bad idea.

Luke caught up with Russell outside the athletic center after the meeting ended. "Hey. About tomorrow night."

"What?" Russell's tone was both bored and confrontational.

"We all know you and Hayden hate each other," Luke said, undeterred. "I don't see why you'd want to go to the cliff with him."

Russell frowned. "I don't."

"So tell Ward," Luke suggested. "He'll go with you. Just tell him you don't want to go with Hayden." It seemed like the perfect solution to Luke. He knew the idea of Hayden and him taking Russell was a bad one. They would fight, and things would go wrong, and Russell might not jump after all, and then there'd be no one to fence on Wednesday.

But Russell merely shrugged. "Why would I do that?"

"Because then you wouldn't have to go with Hayden," Luke explained, frustrated.

"I don't really care who I go with. Applegate, whoever."

"But it would just be so much easier—" Luke pressed.

Russell interrupted him. "What, you don't want to go, is that it? Want to get a good night's sleep before the meet?" he drawled patronizingly. "So don't go. No one's forcing you."

Oh yeah, you and Hayden alone on a cliff. That's a good plan.

"Look, I don't care what you do." Russell said, turning away. "Just as long as I don't have to talk to you." He walked off.

Fine.

Trying not to think too much about all the bad things that might happen on Tuesday, Luke headed off to meet Rachel in the lounge. Yesterday she had mentioned that she was having trouble with her poetry class, and Luke, having taken the class the year before, had offered to help.

She was waiting for him when he arrived. There was no one else there, which wasn't that unusual at this time of day. Midafternoon, most people were outside throwing Frisbees or lazing about on the grass. Luke had actually suggested they study in there instead of outside because he'd known they could be alone.

The lounge was really no more than a dank room in the basement of one of the dorms with a few scattered couches and a stereo. Rachel, in a black tank top and jeans, was sitting at the far end of one of the couches reading her poetry book. Seeing her, Luke felt a wave of panic. Should he sit down next to her or sit on the other end of the couch? He'd like to sit next to her, but what if that was really awkward? But what if he sat down far away, and that was even more awkward? Finally, when he could stand in place no longer, he settled for somewhere in between and plopped himself down. "Hey."

She looked up, smiled. "Hi. I didn't see you come in."

"Uh, yeah." *Say something funny or cool.* "Yep." *Uh-oh. Damage control.* "So what did you say you were having trouble with?" He cleared his throat. "More specifically?"

She showed him the book. "Okay, so it's mainly this scansion stuff. Like finding the stressed and unstressed syllables."

"Yeah, I had trouble with that, too." He thought for a moment. "Sometimes it helps if you tap it out. Like, take the word 'desperate' in the first line of the poem," he said, gesturing to the poetry book. "As you say it, you tap, and you see, you tap harder on the first syllable because that's the stressed one, and the next one's not so hard." He looked at her. "Am I explaining this badly?"

She laughed. "Um . . ."

"Okay, okay. Watch." He tapped his hand on his knee. "DES-per-ate."

"Oh. Okay."

"You try."

"DES-per-ate." She tapped it out on her own knee. "Is that right?"

"Yeah. You know, like, you wouldn't say 'des-PER-ate' or 'des-per-ATE.' It just sounds wrong. Can you hear it?"

Rachel nodded. "I think so."

"Try another one. AN-i-mal."

"AN-i-mal."

Luke smiled. "Good. IS-land."

"IS-land."

"Okay, now a trickier one, and I'm not going to help you," he warned her.

"Not even a little?" she teased.

He grinned. "Nope. Try 'peculiar.'"

"Hey, no fair, that one isn't even in the poem!" she protested.

"That's why it's tricky."

"Cheater."

"Just try it."

"Fine." She got it wrong, accenting the first syllable instead of the second. It frustrated Luke. He could hear it so clearly, and she obviously couldn't. He remembered his poetry teacher saying something about how some people just didn't have the ear for it.

"Try again," he said. "You have to tap it out. Pe-CU-liar." But this time he tapped it out on her knee, not his own. And when he was done, he left his hand there, on her knee.

"Pe-CU-liar," she said correctly, tapping her hand over his on her knee.

"Peculiar," he said, leaning forward and kissing her.

"Peculiar," she said when he finally pulled away. "I think I'm getting the hang of it."

CHAPTER 16

THAT NIGHT Luke entered his room to find Hayden lying flat on his back on the wood floor, eyes squeezed shut, brows knitted tightly together. Luke paused in the doorway. Hayden's arms were folded over his chest, and his dark hair fell over his face.

Luke stared. "What are you doing?"

Hayden's eyes flew open. "Luke!" He stood quickly. "Hey!"

"Hey." Luke entered the room and shut the door behind him. "What's . . . going on?"

Hayden's face turned red. "Nothing, nothing," he said, pushing the hair out of his eyes. "I was just thinking."

"On the floor?"

"I just had to clear my head," Hayden mumbled. "What's the problem?"

Luke shrugged. "I don't know. You just kind of freaked me out a little. Lying there, I mean."

"You got your cliff; I got the floor." He laughed like it was all a big joke.

"It's not *my* cliff," Luke protested.

"Whatever." Hayden sat down on Luke's bed. "So did you get back that bio test you were spazzing out about?"

Subject change. Okay. "Yeah. It was good." Luke leaned back against the door. "It was really good."

"I knew it. You worry too much."

"Yeah."

"Seriously, you do," Hayden said. "And you spend too much time studying for this stuff. It doesn't even really matter."

"Hey, look, just because you can get As without studying doesn't mean the rest of us can."

"I study!"

"Yeah, right," Luke scoffed. "You never study. You don't have to, brainiac."

Hayden laughed. "Fuck you."

"Dork."

"Bitch."

Luke sauntered over to his own bed and sat down facing Hayden. "What'd you do this afternoon?"

"Nothing, just hung out. How'd it go with Rachel?"

Luke's face flushed. "Fine."

Hayden grinned. "Did you . . . ?"

"I kissed her."

"About time."

"Yeah. So what time are we going to the cliff tomorrow night?" Luke asked, suddenly not wanting to talk about Rachel anymore. Just thinking about her made his spine tingle.

Hayden's grin faded. "Late."

"Yeah, but when?"

"I'll tell you when."

Why do you get to make the rules? "Fine." Luke was annoyed. "Maybe I won't even go."

Hayden frowned. "You don't have to go if you don't want to."

"Do you want me to?" *Your call.*

"Yeah," Hayden said. "Go. Otherwise it'll just be me and that piece of shit."

"Maybe we should just let Ward take him," Luke suggested.

"We already said we'd go."

"Yeah, I know, but we could still back out."

"No. We'll do it. We'll just go and get it done."

"Yeah, but why? Why would we want to spend any more time with him than we have to?"

"Hey, it's our squad he's joining," Hayden responded. "So we take him."

"It doesn't *always* happen that way," Luke pointed out.

"Oh my God!" Hayden said, exasperated. "No one's forcing you to go. If you care that much, don't go."

"I don't care that much," muttered Luke.

"Great," Hayden said sarcastically. "Tomorrow night, then."

Luke decided to let it drop. "Whatever. Just let me know when we're going."

"I will." Hayden leaned back on the bed and closed his eyes.

Luke watched him for a second. "See, now you're freaking me out again."

Hayden groaned. "Jesus Christ, Luke. I take a second to think and you go postal."

"Sorry. I guess I'm just not used to you thinking."

"Fuck you."

TUESDAY WENT BY in a blur of classes and tests and homework. When the campus turned black, Hayden, Luke, and Russell made their way through the woods toward the cliff. Luke walked between Russell and Hayden, a somewhat biased buffer. Tonight was important, and he didn't want anything to go wrong. He didn't want them to start fighting. Even though he didn't particularly like Russell, Luke knew that the jump was a special moment, and a part of him felt like it wasn't right for Hayden to spoil it for him.

They reached the cliff's rocky face and climbed together in silence, Hayden taking the lead, Russell in the middle, with Luke trailing slightly behind as they took the path Luke had traveled so many times on his own. They reached the top and stood, looking out over the lake. The moon's reflection glanced off the water and illuminated their faces from below. It reminded Luke of when he and his brother used to hold flashlights under their chins to scare each other.

There was an uneasy pause while Russell stood looking over the edge, Luke and Hayden hanging back a little. Finally, Hayden spoke. "Okay. Jump."

It was so simple a phrase, like that was all there was to it. But Luke understood that to someone who had most likely never jumped off anything so high before, it was much more complicated. Hayden was rushing things, and that wasn't helping.

I should have gotten him not to come. He's just going to mess this up.

When Luke had jumped for the first time, he'd been surrounded by lots of people he knew, people who had also been asked to join the team. The captain at the time, a serious-looking senior called Dan, had had them jump off one by one, and if they balked at the edge, he had other people go first, so that the scared one would have more time to calm down. No one made fun of anyone else. On the cliff with Russell and Hayden, the situation was quite different. There was no safety here tonight.

"We're waiting . . ." said Hayden.

"I'm going!" Russell snapped with a momentary loss of composure. Russell stared over the edge and swallowed hard. His blond hair drifted across his face, pointing downward toward the water.

"Give him a minute," said Luke, and Hayden shot him a glower.

"How high is this thing, anyway?" Russell asked casually.

"High," Hayden said, just as Luke said, "Not high."

Hayden looked at Russell with disgust. "Are you gonna go or not?"

"I said I was going!" Russell said sullenly.

"So why the hell are you still here?" Hayden drawled, sounding bored.

"Give it a rest, Applegate," Russell said bitterly over his shoulder. "It's not like you got somewhere better to be."

"Guys . . ."

"What the *hell* is that supposed to mean?" Hayden barked.

"Well." Russell grinned, knowing he was getting to Hayden. "We all know you don't have a date."

"Excuse me?" Hayden's voice was slippery and deadly, barely audible over the pounding in Luke's head.

"No offense, man." Russell's grin widened, his nervousness momentarily forgotten. "It's just that we all know Nicole has"—he winked—"decided on a little upgrade."

"You fucker!" Hayden started forward menacingly.

"Guys, seriously. Let's just do this and get it over with." Luke tried to sound reasonable, but he came out shrill.

"He's the one who won't jump," Hayden said sulkily, like a kid whose favorite toy had just been confiscated.

"I'm gonna jump," Russell protested.

"Then just jump!" Luke said, frustrated. *I want to go home.*

"He's scared," Hayden crowed. "I knew he was scared!"

"I'm not scared," Russell said coldly.

"Then *go!*" Hayden said. He stepped forward, reaching out with one hand and giving Russell a shove toward the edge of the cliff that hung over the water.

In that moment, time seemed to reduce itself to but a fraction of its speed. Russell's body arched as he stumbled off the edge of the cliff, tumbling backwards—not toward the lake but toward the pointed rocks below.

LUKE WAS FROZEN. His shoulders had clenched pain-
fully, and he felt as if his stomach had fallen out of his body. His
mouth hung open, the back of his throat slightly raw from the loud,
breathy gasp he'd involuntarily made a second earlier. He looked up
at Hayden, who was standing next to him, staring straight ahead at
the place on the cliff where Russell had just been standing.

It was Luke who unsnapped first. He rushed to the edge, kneeling on the cold rock. He squinted fervently downward, unable to
distinguish the dark, swirling water from rock. And body.

Luke bolted away and started back down the cliff. He turned
and noticed Hayden wasn't following. "Come on!" he yelled. Hayden just stood there. "Damn it, Hayden! Move!"

Hayden began to follow Luke down the cliff. Luke rushed forward, the clawing bushes cutting into his arms in shallow scratches.
They reached the edge of the water and Luke waded in, Hayden
hanging back on the bank. It was cold, and soon Luke was up to his
armpits. He shivered as the water seeped into his clothes.

He reached the pointed rocks that jutted out from the cliff
high above and felt his way around them. A cloud had drifted in

front of the moon, and Luke could barely see a foot in front of him. His arms swept over the rocks, searching blindly. "Hayden, help!" he yelled back over his shoulder.

The tops of the rocks were dry, resting a good foot or so above the level of the water, and Luke was startled when he felt a wet rock surface. He pulled away his hand and squinted at it. He could barely see, but it didn't *feel* right. He brought his hand up to his face and sniffed. Metallic. Blood. *Fuck.*

"Russell!" he yelled out into the dark. "Can you hear me?"

He started forward and tripped over something, falling forward and dunking himself underwater. He came up to the surface, gasping. He felt with his foot. Definitely not a rock. He dove under and felt with his hands, and he knew in an instant that it was Russell. He reached his arms around the other boy's stomach and pulled him to the surface. The cloud shifted, and the moon illuminated Russell's motionless face. Blood was oozing from one side of his head. Luke's insides lurched.

Luke began to drag Russell toward the bank. He made it halfway there, and Hayden waded in to help him. In a second, he was beside Luke, grabbing hold of Russell and pulling him onto the sandy shore. Hayden laid Russell out, dropping his head and listening to Russell's mouth as Luke sloshed out of the water.

"He's not breathing," Hayden said quietly.

Luke collapsed next to Russell and put his hand in front of Russell's nose. There was no airflow. "Shit!" He opened Russell's mouth with his hands. He froze. What now? He didn't know CPR. He'd seen it in movies, sure, but it involved pressing on someone's rib cage and what if he broke something or made it worse?

"Luke . . ." Hayden whispered.

Luke turned to Hayden. "Call an ambulance!" He could hear Hayden fumble in his pockets for his phone and start to dial.

Luke made a decision. He clasped his left hand tightly over his right and pushed down hard, rhythmically, on Russell's stomach. *One, two, three, four, five. One, two, three, four, five. Just like they do on TV.* But this was the part where a spray of water was supposed to come from Russell's mouth, and he was supposed to turn over and cough. And he didn't.

Maybe Luke was supposed to blow air into Russell's mouth. He'd seem them do that on TV. He moved toward Russell, then pulled back, suddenly squeamish. He didn't want to put his mouth on Russell's. That was disgusting! But he forced himself to pull Russell's bloody lips apart with his hand and cover Russell's mouth with his own and blow as hard as he could.

One, two, three, four, five, blow. One, two, three, four, five, blow. One, two, three, four, five, blow. Come on. Breathe. Come on. Please, please, please, breathe.

He was still trying when the ambulance arrived. He was still screaming "Breathe!" to Russell when the paramedics pulled him away to wait by Hayden, who was sitting, rocking slightly on the bank.

Luke watched, dazed, as the paramedics put an oxygen mask on Russell's face and listened for a heartbeat, checked for a pulse. The two paramedics shouted things at each other, things Luke didn't understand, until finally one of them turned to the other and said, "Call it."

Call what?

The other paramedic checked his watch and said something softly that Luke couldn't hear. Or didn't want to hear.

The first paramedic approached Hayden and Luke. "I'm sorry to have to tell you this."

I'm sorry to have to tell you this. The words echoed through Luke's head. The same words that had shattered his whole world once before. He had a desperate urge to clamp his hand over the man's mouth, to make him start the sentence over, as if its beginning could somehow influence the message that had to be conveyed.

"Your friend is dead."

Luke knew it was coming, but it shook him all the same. He leaned over and slammed his head into the sand, retching emptily and gasping for breath. He could feel the paramedic's hand on his back, heard the words "I'm so sorry." It meant nothing.

He collapsed onto his side, the gritty sand pushing against his head. This wasn't happening. It couldn't be happening. Around him, Luke could hear the sounds of the lake and the paramedics moving around him. Next to him, he could hear Hayden's voice, saying quietly and almost calmly, "I killed him. Oh God. I killed him."

CHAPTER 19

LUKE SPENT THE REST of the night at the police station, giving his statement. The detectives he spoke to told him he could hire a lawyer. He refused. *Just tell them the truth, and it'll be fine. Just tell them the truth, and they'll let you go home.*

Two detectives brought him into a small holding room furnished only with a chair and a table. On one of the walls, there was a large mirror. Luke knew he was being watched.

Both detectives were tall, thin men in their early forties, and soon their names and faces had blended together until they seemed to Luke like one entity. Their questions shot out at him like bullets, and Luke answered monotonously and unemotionally. He was too tired to think, too tired to plan out what to say.

"What were you doing on the cliff?"

"Russell was going to jump."

"Why was Russell going to jump?"

"To join the team."

"Why would Russell have to jump to join the team?"

"I don't know."

"Did anyone else know you were up there?"

"Our teammates."

"Is Hayden your friend?"

"Yes."

"Was Russell your friend?"

"No."

Luke responded without making eye contact, staring straight ahead at the wall behind the detectives. He just wanted it all to be over. He hadn't had time to process what had happened yet, and the last thing he wanted right now was to be bombarded with questions. He wanted to go home, go to sleep, and have it all be a dream in the morning.

"Did Russell jump?"

"Russell fell."

"Why did Russell fall?"

"I don't know."

"Did someone push him?"

"I don't know."

"Did you push him?"

"No."

"Did Hayden push him?"

"I don't know."

The detectives seemed disgusted with Luke's noncommittal responses, but Luke was trying the best he could. Everything was so jumbled up in his head. He didn't know what was going on. He didn't know what the right answers were.

"Did Hayden hit Russell?"

"No."

"At any point in time, did Hayden touch him?"

"Yes."

"Where did Hayden touch him?

"His shoulder."

"When did he touch him?"

"Before he fell."

"Right before Russell fell?"

"Yes."

"Did you touch Russell?"

"No."

Every question Luke answered made him feel like he was doing something wrong. He was sure he was messing it all up. He wanted to take a break. He asked, but they wouldn't let him. They had more questions. They kept asking about Hayden.

"Did Hayden and Russell like each other?"

"No."

"Why not?"

"I don't know."

"Was Hayden angry with Russell?"

"I don't know."

"Does Hayden get angry a lot?"

"I don't know."

"Does Hayden ever hit people?"

"I don't know."

The detectives seemed to know things they shouldn't. Luke didn't understand how they got all their information. They just seemed to know. *Hayden is probably telling them,* Luke guessed. He wished he could hear what his friend was saying. He wished Hayden could come tell him what to say.

"Who is Nicole Johnston?"

"A girl at school."

"Russell's girlfriend?"

"Yes."

"Did she used to go out with Hayden?"

"Yes."

"Is that why Russell and Hayden didn't like each other?"

"I don't know."

"Did you like Russell?"

"No."

"Why not?"

"I don't know."

"Are you sorry he's dead?"

"Yes!"

"Do you think Hayden is?"

"Yes!"

Luke's mouth became dry, and he asked the detectives if he could have a glass of water. They told him no. He didn't press it.

"Why were you and Hayden there with Russell?"

"To see him jump."

"Did you volunteer to be there?"

"Hayden did."

"Why?"

"I don't know."

"Did you want to be there?"

"I don't know."

"Did you think Hayden should be there?"

"I don't know."

"Did you tell Hayden you didn't know if he should be there?"

"Yes."

"But he insisted?"

"Yes."

"Why do you think he did that?"

"I don't know."

They asked him the same questions over and over again. Sometimes Luke couldn't remember the answers he'd given the first time. Most of the questions weren't about him. Most of the questions were about Hayden.

"Did Hayden use force when he touched Russell?"

"I don't know."

"Did he shove him?"

"I don't know."

"Did Hayden shove him off the cliff?"

"I don't know."

"Did Hayden kill Russell?"

"I don't know."

The detectives made Luke write it all down and sign it. An affidavit, they called it. After a few hours, they told him he could go back to school. He asked them if they were going to arrest him. They asked, "Should we?"

"What about Hayden?" Luke said. "Is he going back, too?"

"No," one of the detectives said. "We still have a few more questions to ask your friend. We had to wait until his lawyer got here before we could talk to him. It'll take a little longer."

"But then he can go home?" Luke asked.

The detective shrugged. "Depends."

"Is he under arrest?"

"We're just asking him some more questions," the detective answered simply. "We're trying to figure out what happened."

Me too. "What did he say?"

The detective stared at him for a moment. "Well, he said you had nothing to do with Russell falling, if that's what you're wondering." He looked at Luke as if he were something he'd scraped off the bottom of his shoe. "He said you never touched the guy. That's what you're worried about, isn't it?"

"N-no!" Luke stammered. "I mean, I just—"

"Go home," the detective said. "An officer will drive you."

CHAPTER 20

WHEN LUKE GOT BACK to Briar Academy, Headmaster Arthur Grunberg was waiting for him in the front hall. The old man brought Luke up to his office, where Luke had been only once before, on the night his father had died. They stood there together for a moment, each unsure of what to say.

"Tonight," the headmaster wheezed, "was a very difficult night."

"Yeah," Luke mumbled.

"If you want to talk about what happened—"

"No!" Luke cut him off, then felt embarrassed. "I don't mean to be rude. It's just . . . been a long night."

Headmaster Grunberg nodded. "Yes. Well. I've spoken to your mother."

"Oh."

"She's expecting your phone call, so I'll let you . . ." The old man gestured to the phone on the desk. "Take your time," he said, hobbling toward the door. He turned back. "She's worried sick about you."

I'll bet.

Because he could think of nothing else to do, Luke dialed, and his mother picked up after the second ring. "Luke?"

"Hi," he said stupidly.

"Luke, what happened?" His mother's voice came over the line shrill and panicky. "Mr. Grunberg told me that a boy died? That you were involved?"

"Yeah." Luke's throat stiffened. "A guy from school. There was an accident."

"What kind of accident, Luke?"

"He fell?" It wasn't supposed to be a question.

"From what?"

"A cliff."

"There are cliffs at your school?" Luke's mother asked incredulously.

"Just one," Luke responded. *No more questions. I want to go to sleep. Just let me sleep.*

"Well, what has it got to do with you?" Luke's mother demanded.

"I was there. When he fell. I was standing right next to him."

"Oh my God."

"Yeah." *I'm surprised you care.*

"Why were you standing next to a boy on a cliff? Did you . . . Did you do something, Luke?"

Never mind. "I didn't kill him if that's what you mean!" Luke snapped.

"I'm sorry. I didn't mean it like that. I'm sorry. I just—I'm trying to understand what happened. I mean, for God's sake, Luke, you just told me you watched another boy fall off a cliff!"

"Well, I'm sorry this is so difficult for *you!*" Luke shot back.

There was a pause. "Okay." His mother sounded like she was scrambling to find the right words. "Okay, look, let's . . . let's be reasonable. Do I need to hire you a lawyer?"

"No."

"What do you mean no? Are they charging you with anything?"

"I don't know. I don't think so."

"Still," she said, "I should probably hire you a lawyer. Edward Learner, he's the best. I'll call him tonight."

"No, don't. Don't hire anyone. They haven't even arrested me. I don't need a lawyer."

"Of course you need a lawyer, Luke. You spoke to the police!"

"Well, I don't want one."

Luke's mother sighed. "Don't be ridiculous, Luke. I'm calling Edward. He's the absolute best."

"Jesus fucking Christ, Mom! I'm eighteen—it's my call! And I said that I don't want a fucking lawyer!" Luke screamed into the phone.

For a long time, there was silence. Then, "Clearly, you're upset."

Luke leaned back against the headmaster's desk, exhausted. "Yeah. Yeah, I'm upset."

"I want to help you."

"Great."

"Tell me what to do, Luke," she said. "What do you want me to do? You don't want me to call a lawyer, fine. Just . . . tell me what you want me to do."

"I don't want anything from you."

"I'm going to drive up there. In the morning. Or I can come now."

"No. Don't." *Too much. I can't handle this. Too much.*

"It's not a problem. I can get into my car right now. I'm going to the garage. I'll be there in a few hours."

"No, just don't. Stop."

"But I—"

"Don't."

"But don't you want to come home?" His mother's voice sounded very small.

"No," he said firmly.

"Are you sure?"

"Very." And without waiting for his mother to say another word, Luke hung up the phone.

CHAPTER 21

LUKE HAD BEEN HALFWAY through his first year at Briar before he ever saw the cliff. It had been Hayden's idea to go check it out. They'd joined the JV team a few weeks before and had heard about the initiation process. "We should get a sense of it," Hayden had decided. "So we'll be ready."

Luke had never had a problem with heights, but he got a little nervous when he saw the cliff. It was pretty steep, and Luke had learned enough about surface tension to know that a belly flop off the top would *hurt.* He wondered if a varsity letter was worth that.

"You'd think more people would come up here," Hayden pondered when they'd climbed to the top. "Great view, you know?"

"Maybe they're afraid of falling?" Luke suggested, looking skeptically down toward the water. "I doubt I'll be jumping anytime soon," he said, partly just to reassure himself. "I'm nowhere near varsity level."

"Me neither," said Hayden. "But we're getting there. We just need to practice more."

"Yeah." Luke traced a rock with the tip of his sneaker. He thought they were practicing a lot already.

"I've been thinking about this," Hayden continued, "and I think it's a matter of getting some more time in the gym. So we'll do like a couple times a week during free periods. I think it'll make a real difference."

"Okay."

"And we'll have a little less work to do next term, too, remember." Hayden had decided they'd take the notoriously mellow drama class and the easiest of the English electives during second term. (It was one of the best parts about being friends with Hayden: you didn't have to stress out over things like course selection.)

"You'll probably make varsity before I do," Luke said. "This stuff comes way easier to you."

Hayden glowed, as he always did when flattered, but then his face turned serious. "We have to make the team together. 'Cause it'll be much better that way."

Luke cracked up. "You don't like to do *anything* alone, do you?"

His best friend grinned. "Nope."

Luke walked over to the edge of the cliff. "We just jump off right here?" He lay flat on the rocks with his head over the edge. He looked down. "That's high, though."

Hayden joined him. "Yeah."

"So everyone on varsity has done this?" Luke asked.

"That's what Dan said."

"What happens if you hit those rocks down there?"

Hayden laughed. "Nobody hits the rocks."

"How do you know?"

"Because if people hit the rocks, nobody would ever do it."

"Good point," Luke had said.

CHAPTER 22

THE DAY AFTER Russell died, Luke woke up alone in his dorm room. It took a moment for everything to sink in. It all still felt like a dream, as if it had never really happened. He half expected Hayden to come in the door and rag on him for sleeping so late. But the room was still. Hayden wasn't coming.

Hayden is in jail.

Russell is dead.

Luke rubbed the sleep from his eyes and ran his hand over the back of his neck. He got dressed and debated going down to the dining hall to get lunch. He decided against it. People would have heard by now. They'd know what had happened to Russell. They'd know what Luke had done, seen, been a part of. They'd look at him differently.

Someone knocked on the door. *Should I answer it? What if it's someone wanting to ask me more questions?*

"Luke? It's me, Rachel. Are you awake?"

Shit. Luke eyed himself in the mirror, saw how awful he looked, and groaned inwardly. Then he opened the door. Rachel stood there, wearing jeans and a bulky gray sweatshirt. Her hair was pulled back into a ponytail. She still looked stunning. "You look like crap," she stated, pushing past him into the room. She flopped down onto Hayden's bed. "I heard about what happened. There was an announcement this morning."

"Fantastic," Luke drawled.

She frowned. "Um. Yeah, well. Are you okay?"

Something twisted inside Luke. "That's why you're here. To find out if I'm okay. How nice."

Rachel paused. "Right. Well. I just thought maybe . . ." She let it trail off, but when Luke stared at her, she finished the sentence awkwardly: ". . . you wanted someone to talk to."

Luke raised an eyebrow. "Talk about what?"

"I don't know. Anything. I mean, what happened was really intense. I mean, Russell . . . My God, you know?"

"Did you know him?"

"Not really," she admitted.

"Then I'm so sorry for your loss," he spat out pointedly.

Rachel's eyes widened. "Jesus, Luke, I was just trying to—"

"To what? Get all the juicy details? So you can go back and tell your friends all about it?" Luke asked, eyes blazing.

She looked shocked. "No, I just—"

Luke walked toward her. "You just wanted to know, so I'll tell you."

"No, Luke, it's not like that."

"No, you wanted to know, so I'll tell you," he hissed, standing in front of the bed and leering down at her. "I'll tell you every fucking detail. That'll make you happy. You want to know about the look on Russell's face?"

Rachel shook her head. "No." She inched away from him, scared.

He leaned forward, forcing her farther backwards, until she was almost flat on her back on the bed. "Oh yeah, I'll bet you do. But do you want to know about it before, on the cliff? Or after, in the water, when he was covered in blood?"

"Luke!"

"Yeah, I could tell you about it." He shrugged. "Make your story a hell of a lot better, wouldn't it?"

Rachel looked like she was about to cry. "Why are you acting like this?"

Luke froze. *Why am I acting like this?* He straightened and took a step back. "Maybe you should go."

Her eyes narrowed. "You think?" She stood up and crossed the room quickly, almost running to the door. "God, you are such an asshole. And here I was trying to help you!"

You're right. Fuck, you're right.

She cast him a venomous look. "I can't believe I ever liked you," she said, and she left.

Luke stood facing the door for a long time after Rachel left. "I fucked that up," he muttered. "I really fucked that up." He took a deep breath in through his nose and held it for a second. Then he let it out. *What the hell do I do now?*

He didn't go to class, but he doubted anyone expected him to. He just sat in the room, not really thinking, not really doing much of anything. He wanted to wake up. He wanted it all to be a bad dream. He must have dozed off, because the next thing he knew it was evening. A knocking at his door had awoken him. He answered it with dread. There was absolutely no one he wanted to talk to right now.

Drew, Freddy, and Courtney were standing in the hallway. They entered without waiting to be invited. "Oh my God, Luke," said Courtney. She lurched forward and wrapped her arms around him. Luke was too startled to return the hug. His arms hung limply at his sides, and after a moment she stepped back. "Are you traumatized? Oh my God."

Drew stepped past her to close the door to the room. He turned back and settled with Freddy on Hayden's bed. Luke felt like saying, "You have no right!" but he wasn't sure what he meant.

"This is crazy," said Freddy. "Everyone's talking. They're saying that Hayden's in jail. They're saying that Russell's dead. Grunberg made a speech."

"Oh my God," Courtney contributed.

All three turned to Luke, waiting. Clearly they expected him to tell them everything. The fact that he'd been holed up in his room for an entire day, not wanting to see anyone, didn't seem to bother them. They couldn't fathom that that applied to them.

"It's true." Luke tried to keep his voice calm. He didn't want to yell at them like he had at Rachel. He couldn't afford to lose any more friends. But seeing their eyes watching him greedily, he couldn't help but hate them.

"What's true?" Courtney pushed. "Luke, what happened?"

"I don't want to talk about it."

"Luke, you have to tell us what happened," Freddy almost lectured. "They're saying Hayden *killed* Russell!"

"Is that what they're saying?" Luke felt a numbness spread from his feet to his face.

"What *happened?*" Courtney asked again.

"I don't want to talk about it."

"But we're your *friends,*" Freddy said.

"My friends," Luke repeated.

Drew spoke up from across the room. "What happened to Russell?"

Luke turned to look at him. "Russell is dead." *Russell is dead. Russell is dead. Russell is dead.*

"But how did he die?" asked Drew. "Did Hayden really kill him?"

"Guys—" said Luke. "Guys, can you just . . ."

"What?" Courtney leaned forward like a vulture.

"Can you just *go?*"

They stared at him. "Luke." Freddy sounded hurt.

Suddenly there was another knock at the door. *I'm so popular today,* Luke thought darkly. He moved past Courtney to open the door. Headmaster Grunberg was standing on the other side. "Luke," the old man said. Then he caught sight of the other three. "Well, hello."

"We were just—" Courtney stammered.

"We wanted to make sure Luke was okay," said Freddy.

Bullshit, thought Luke. *Maybe Rachel wanted to see if I was okay. You were here for the story.*

"Mm," said the headmaster. He didn't step into the room. Instead, he stood staring, almost glaring, really, at Drew and Freddy and Courtney.

"Well, we'll just go, then," Freddy said uncertainly. "Let us know if, you know . . ." he said to Luke.

"Yeah."

After they were gone, the headmaster came into the room. He looked instantly out of place. Luke suddenly felt embarrassed. If he'd known the old man was coming, he might have cleaned up a little. At least he would have picked up all the clothes on the floor. "I thought I'd come and see how you were doing," the headmaster said.

Luke shrugged. "I'm okay."

"As you may already know, I've spoken to the student body." He grimaced. "So I want you to know that you don't have to talk about it. If you don't want to."

"Oh."

"Unless you'd like to," he clarified.

"No."

The headmaster nodded. "Is your mother coming?"

"No."

"Ah. Well. Have you given any thought to whether you'd like to go home?"

Luke shrugged again. "I'd rather stay here."

"Okay." The headmaster gestured toward the desk chair. "Do you mind if I . . . ?"

"No," Luke said. "Go ahead."

The headmaster sat down in the chair slowly, holding his back. "I met with Russell's parents today," he informed Luke. "And Hayden's."

"Is he coming back?" Luke asked. "Hayden, I mean."

"That's what I've come to tell you," said the old man. "He's been arrested. Premeditated murder."

What? "But it was an accident!" Luke sputtered. "I mean, we screwed up, it was stupid, but it was an accident!"

"The police don't seem to think so," the headmaster said sadly. "Since Hayden is eighteen, he'll be tried as an adult. It would have been easier if he were a few months younger, but . . ." The old man sighed.

Luke sat down across from the headmaster on Hayden's bed. "They're arresting him." The words didn't make sense.

"Yes."

"Is there going to be a trial?"

"I believe so."

"Jesus Christ." Luke stared down at his bare feet. "Can Hayden come home? Before the trial, I mean."

"Well, there'll be a hearing for bail, I think. But Hayden's father told me that the lawyer said, well, with the financial status of Hayden's family, he's considered a flight risk. Bail isn't likely." The old man rubbed his eye with the back of his gnarled, spotted hand. "I'm sorry."

"Yeah."

The old man shifted uncomfortably in the chair. "The district attorney called. This morning. She wants to speak with you."

Luke looked up. "Are they arresting me, too?" *Oh God, oh God, oh God.*

"No, she just wants to talk to you about what happened. I imagine . . . I imagine she'll want you to testify. As the only eyewitness."

"I already talked to the police," Luke protested.

"I know, but I think this is different."

"Yeah."

"Also," said Headmaster Grunberg, "you should know, students are now banned from going anywhere near the cliff."

"Oh."

"I suppose it doesn't make too much of a difference now." For a couple of minutes, the two sat there in silence, looking at anything but each other: the floor, the clothes, the bed, the desk. "Luke," the headmaster said. "I know this is exceedingly difficult. I can only imagine . . . I think you should meet with Dr. Locke."

"The guidance counselor?"

"It might be good for you to be able to say what you need to. These next few months are going to be very trying."

Luke reddened. "Thanks, but I don't really think that's . . . right for me." After his father's death, Luke's mother had decided that he and Jason should meet with a therapist. Both brothers had had to spend one awkward hour a week talking with a frustratingly nice and altogether unhelpful woman who insisted that they'd feel so much better if they could only "let go." After a month of anxiously lying to his friends about where he was disappearing to every Thursday afternoon, Luke flat-out refused to go anymore. Jason stuck it out only a little while longer.

"Just consider it. Will you do that for me?" Luke nodded reluctantly, and the headmaster stood up. "I'll leave you the number of the district attorney. You should call her soon." He dropped a piece of paper on the desk. He looked around the room, then back at Luke. "This whole thing . . . I've been headmaster of this school for thirty years, and nothing's ever . . ." He coughed briskly into his hand, shook his head, and left.

And alone, as the quiet settled around him, Luke began to cry. His tears rolled down his face, and soon the bedspread was wet and his chest was shaking and the images and memories were blaring through his brain. Soundless, muffled by the pillow he clasped over his head, he sobbed.

All the while, Russell's last words burned into Luke's mind, leaving charred destruction in their wake. "I'm not scared."

"I am," Luke whispered.

CHAPTER 23

DISTRICT ATTORNEY Angela Garvey was a short, thin woman in her early thirties. She had whitish-blond hair, slicked back flat on top of her head and pulled tightly into a bun, and large blue eyes framed by long lashes. She was pretty in a creepy sort of way, with a small mouth and abnormally high cheekbones. From the moment he entered her office, Luke was sure they were not going to get along.

Angela Garvey flashed Luke a wide smile and gestured for him to sit in the black leather chair in front of her desk. "Good morning, Luke," she said. "Mind if I call you Luke?" Her voice was crisp and brittle.

Luke shrugged. "No, go ahead." *Let's just get this meeting over with.*

"Excellent." Ms. Garvey had a way of over-enunciating her words, so that each hard consonant sound seemed to reverberate around the room. She sat down in her swiveling desk chair and leaned across the desk toward Luke. "It's a terrible thing that happened to your friend," she said. "A young man, dying like that." She shook her head remorsefully.

Russell wasn't my friend. "Yeah." Luke couldn't help feeling like he should be on guard, like the district attorney was preparing to launch an attack.

"I understand the funeral's tomorrow," she said.

"Yeah."

"I appreciate you taking the time to meet with me. I can only imagine what this must be like for you," Ms. Garvey told him. "I mean, one friend brutally murdering another. And you having to watch that, see it happen, and be unable to stop it." She shook her head again. "A terrible thing."

"It wasn't like that," Luke said. "It was an accident."

"Are you sure?" Ms. Garvey asked, pointing her blue eyes directly at Luke. "Are you absolutely positive? Because that's what you'd have to be to let someone get away with murder."

Hayden's not a murderer.

"Look at the facts, Luke. Hayden hated Russell. He made threatening comments to him only weeks before his death. Then he insisted he be the one to take Russell to the cliff, even though you tried to dissuade him. And as soon as Russell's back was to the edge, Hayden pushed him." Ms. Garvey didn't break eye contact. "You and I both know Hayden's got a temper."

This sounds wrong.

"Can you honestly look me in the eye, Luke, and tell me that you are one hundred percent sure that Hayden Applegate didn't mean to push Russell Conrad to his death?"

Can I?

"I didn't think so."

Luke said nothing. He kicked the heels of his shoes against his leather chair.

Ms. Garvey exhaled loudly. "The fact of the matter is that Russell Conrad is dead. And Hayden Applegate is responsible. You and I both know this, Luke. That's a fact. That's the *truth.*" She leaned back in her chair. "I just want to be sure that when you're put up on that stand to testify, you're going to tell the *truth.*"

"I'll tell it like I saw it." *How did I see it?*

Ms. Garvey frowned. "You're going to have to give me a little more than that, Luke. A boy is dead. I understand that Hayden is your friend, but think about this." She leaned forward in her chair again. "Russell Conrad is not going home tonight. Or any other night. He's never going to talk to his parents again, or go to school, or hang out with friends, or fight with his little sister. Hayden Applegate took his life from him. And if you let Hayden walk away, Luke, can you live with that?"

Jesus. "It's not up to me," Luke said, trying to convince himself as much as the lawyer. "The jury will decide."

"I'm going to be honest with you, Luke. Your testimony's going to matter a lot. You were the only one who saw what happened, and the only one who can tell the *truth,* that Hayden murdered Russell in cold blood. You saw it."

"Don't tell me what I saw; I know what I saw!" Luke snapped.

The district attorney nodded. "All right. You take some time to think things through. I'm not trying to push you."

Bullshit.

"I like you, Luke. I really do. And I want to help you. You just have to let me." She sighed. "Luke, let's talk about that night."

"I already told everything to the police," Luke retorted. His dislike for her was growing by the second.

"Right." She opened up a file on her desk. "You told the detectives that Hayden *intentionally* shoved Russell, is that correct?"

"It's what I said."

"And that was why Russell fell," she supplied.

"I didn't say that," Luke argued. "That's not in your little file."

"But it's the *truth,* Luke," the district attorney asked. "Isn't it?"

Luke hesitated. "I don't know."

"Yes, you do." Angela Garvey smiled. "Yes, you do, Luke."

He got up and left. He knew it was rude, but he just couldn't be there any longer. He didn't wait to see the surprised look on her face as he walked out. He didn't stop when she called out to him that they weren't finished. The meeting was over. It had to be over. It was just too much for him right now.

CHAPTER 24

LUKE KEPT SEEING HAYDEN out of the corner of his eye. In their dorm room, every time he turned around, Hayden was on the bed or at the desk or lying on the floor with his eyes shut like Luke had found him the day before Russell died. And even when Luke didn't outright *see* him, there were little mind triggers everywhere: Hayden's clothes on the floor, his posters on the walls, his sandals by the door. It had never been Luke's room. From the very beginning, it had been Luke and Hayden's.

It felt wrong to be there alone—it felt wrong to be there at all—but it was so hard to be outside of the room. Everyone stared.

Luke started going to class again. No one talked to him, and he didn't talk to anyone. Even the teachers seemed wary of him. His Spanish teacher, Señora Levine, had actually screamed once, when she entered the classroom a little early and found Luke waiting there for class to begin. She recovered quickly, mumbling something about how he'd startled her, but the message was clear. People were afraid of him.

There were whispers, of course, and he heard them. Nothing so dramatic had ever happened in Briar Academy's history. A student falling to his death! Possibly pushed! Though only Hayden and not Luke had been charged with Russell's murder, the rest of the student body failed to see this distinction. From the bits of conversation Luke caught before his classmates would abruptly silence themselves, Luke was able to hear perfectly clearly that they suspected him of being just as guilty.

His first fencing practice after Russell's death was one of the worst experiences of his life. He'd gotten there early, not wanting to enter into a room full of people. What he didn't anticipate, though, was that each fencer, upon entering the gym, would stare at him, freeze, and then keep walking. Drew and Freddy came in together, and for a moment it looked to Luke like Freddy was going to say something to him. But maybe he imagined it, because after a moment they both just walked away.

Luke hadn't spoken to Drew, Freddy, or Courtney since that awful afternoon in his dorm room. Whenever he saw them and tried to make eye contact, they cast him unsettled looks and turned away. Eventually he'd just stopped trying.

Making an effort to ignore his teammates' stares and silent treatment, Luke focused on his dummy work. He was still attempting to perfect his draw cut, but every time he tried to picture how it was supposed to look, he saw Russell's wrist twisting and the blade skimming flawlessly across the dummy's surface. Luke switched to four cuts.

The sophomores joined him timidly after a few minutes, and it took Luke a moment to realize, *This is my entire squad.* Technically, with Hayden gone, it was Luke's job to lead it. But Alex and Ben didn't seem to need a squad leader. They practiced together, switching from dummy work to cuff cuts and round-the-clock parries. Without a partner, Luke stayed on the dummy. They didn't invite him to switch in with them, and he didn't ask.

As he watched, Alex made a head cut, raising his arm high and leaving half his body vulnerable. *I won't say anything. Who cares?* Alex did it again, this time locking his arm and bouncing his sword clumsily against Ben's mask. *Ben should say something. Maybe he doesn't notice.* This was usually the time when Hayden would step in. "It's not good to practice bad habits," he always said. "They stick, and then we're all screwed."

"Alex," Luke said. Both boys reeled around. "You're raising your arm."

"Oh," the younger boy said. "Okay. Thanks."

Luke nodded and watched as Alex tried the cut again. "Better," he said, though it wasn't quite right. "You're still kind of locking your elbow, though." This felt wrong. Luke shouldn't be giving advice like this. He wasn't a squad leader. That was Hayden's job, not his. He wished he'd never said anything. He wished he'd never come back to practice. He wished he'd never learned to fence.

"Is that better?" Alex asked.

Luke hadn't seen it. "I don't know," he said, harsher than he'd intended. Alex flinched. Luke turned back to his dummy, trying to forget that the sophomores were even there.

When Coach Dawson arrived, he looked just as surprised as everyone else to see Luke. He crossed the room with a small wave and a funny smile. "You're back," he said, with forced enthusiasm.

"Uh, yeah." *I'm not sure why, now.*

"You know, Luke, if you wanted to take some time off . . . I mean, everyone would understand . . ." Five minutes later Luke ducked out of practice and went back to his room. Fencing was over. He was done.

He wasn't sure who he could talk to. Rachel hadn't spoken to him since that day last week in his room. He didn't blame her. His mother was impossible to discuss anything with. Jason probably couldn't care less. Hayden was in jail. Luke turned to his last option. The headmaster had suggested he talk to the school's guidance counselor. Luke finally agreed.

CHAPTER 25

LUKE WASN'T EXACTLY SURE what to expect when he walked into Dr. Locke's office. There was truly only one word that could describe the office: small. It had once been the janitor's closet. A desk was shoved into the far corner of the closet, with a chair behind it and a second chair of a foamier quality in front of it, so close that when Luke sat down in it, his knees brushed against the cold wood of the desk.

The room was dimly lit, but Luke could still make out Dr. Locke's round, young face beaming back at him. Dr. Locke was overweight, balding early with a comb-over. A chubby face thrust out from his plain suit, resting upon a neck like a tree trunk. On first glance, it looked as if the doctor's mouth had swallowed his nose. "I want you to feel like you can talk to me," he was saying.

This sounds so fake. "Uh . . . yeah, sure." *Maybe this was a bad idea.*

"And we can talk about whatever you want to talk about. Whatever's on your mind."

This was definitely a bad idea.

"You can tell me what's going on, and together we can work on it. Okay, Lucas?"

"I go by Luke," he said sharply.

Dr. Locke blinked. "What?"

"Nobody calls me Lucas. Everybody calls me Luke." His voice was cold.

"Ah, yes. Of course. Well, why don't you tell me what's on your mind?"

Maybe because you're a bad counselor. "I don't know." Luke folded his arms. *I need to leave.*

"That's okay. How about we just talk about how you're feeling?"

"How I'm feeling?" Luke had to clarify that he had heard correctly. It was just such a stupid question. Did Dr. Locke really expect him to sit here and talk to a total stranger about his *feelings?* Then again, wasn't that why he'd come in the first place? To talk? But Luke didn't feel like talking anymore. Now he just wanted to get out. The whole meeting seemed entirely useless.

"Yes, how are you?" Dr. Locke repeated.

"Fine, thank you. How are you?" Luke said automatically, then caught himself and blushed.

Dr. Locke looked a little taken aback. He swallowed hard, his Adam's apple jutting out from his thick neck. "What I meant was, how are you dealing with things?"

Luke slouched in his seat, assuming the I'm-just-a-screwed-up-teenager-that-you-should-write-off-right-now-and-let-me-get-out-of-here pose, the one that helped you get out of serious trouble. The one that Hayden had taught him. "Okay," Luke said, simply and casually, his voice taking on a nonchalant tone that he hoped would satisfy Dr. Locke. After all, the guy didn't exactly seem like a rocket scientist.

The guidance counselor frowned, his bushy eyebrows meeting in the middle of his forehead under his round-rimmed glasses. "If you were having trouble, after everything, that would be all right, you know," Dr. Locke said.

I'm glad I have your permission.

"What I mean is, it's completely normal."

Nothing about this is normal.

"I noticed that you didn't go to Russell's funeral," the doctor attempted.

Luke shrugged. "My alarm didn't go off."

Dr. Locke leaned forward in his office chair. "How about the truth," he said, assuming his I-understand-more-than-you-think-I-do-because-I'm-a-smart-ass-prick pose.

"That *is* the truth. I'm thinking of getting a new clock at RadioShack, " Luke said with an attempt at carelessness. Dr. Locke was sweating and looked very uncomfortable. "Fuckin' Sony," Luke added for good measure.

Dr. Locke hemmed and hawed a bit, then looked Luke in the eye. "I don't remember seeing you at the school's memorial either. It was a moving event. The student body really came together."

Luke said nothing.

"Did your alarm clock not go off then?"

"Forgot to set it."

"I see." Dr. Locke frowned.

"Yeah." Luke tugged at the collar of his button-down shirt. His sleeves were rolled up just above his elbows. The shirt was stiff and constricting, not like the T-shirts he usually wore, but he hadn't done laundry in a while, so the shirt was all he had. It took him a moment to realize that it was the same shirt he'd worn to dinner at his mother's.

Dr. Locke adjusted his tie and pressed on valiantly. "And have you been to jail to see Hayden?"

"I don't want to talk about Hayden," Luke said.

Dr. Locke smiled wanly. "All right, Luke. What should we talk about instead?"

"I don't know," Luke said.

The guidance counselor clasped his hands in front of him. "In order for me to help you, you have to let me," he said.

"Yeah, I can see how this is going to be a *big* help!" Luke stood up, shoving his chair behind him. His dramatic exit was only marred by the fact that he tripped trying to climb over the arm of the foamy chair on his way out of the janitor's closet.

CHAPTER 26

LUKE HALF WALKED, half ran away from Dr. Locke's office, opening the door out of the building with such force that it slammed into the person on the other side. Luke was in the middle of a rushed apology when he realized the person he'd crashed the door into was Tristan.

Tristan was still on crutches, and it took a few minutes for Luke to help him to his feet. "I'm really sorry about that," Luke mumbled.

"It's all right," Tristan said with a shrug.

"I just had to get out of there," Luke said vaguely.

"Visiting Dr. Locke?" Tristan asked.

"Yeah," Luke responded, ready to defend himself.

Tristan nodded. "Yeah, I'm on my way there."

"Wouldn't bother," Luke offered. "He's pretty useless."

"Is he?" Tristan sounded disappointed. "That's annoying."

"Yeah."

"Felt like I needed someone to talk to, you know? With everything that happened." He paused. "I mean, I know it's way harder for you," he added quickly.

"I guess," said Luke.

"Rachel said you were pretty . . . upset."

Luke felt humiliated. Rachel had talked to Tristan about the way he'd acted. "I was an idiot."

"Yeah, that's more like what she said," Tristan replied. He looked a little angry at Luke, but he was still trying to be nice.

"I should apologize to her."

"Maybe you should leave her alone for a while," Tristan suggested.

"Oh. She doesn't want to talk to me."

"Well, I mean, she didn't say that, but she's kind of angry now, and maybe if you wait a little . . ."

"Right," Luke said, leaning back against the door he'd just come out of. "All this, it's crazy, isn't it?"

"Unreal," Tristan agreed. "I mean, just . . . the way they're trying to fuck up Hayden's life."

"What?"

"These lawyers and shit. It's unreal."

Luke swallowed, uncomfortable. "Well, I mean, Hayden kind of fucked up his own life, didn't he?" Tristan raised an eyebrow. "And I mean, Russell's life is just *over*."

"So Hayden's life should be over, too?"

"Hey, you weren't there," Luke said defensively.

"Are you saying he did it on purpose?" Tristan demanded.

"I didn't say that."

"I thought you were his friend."

"I am his friend. I just think it's more complicated than that."

"No, Luke, it's not. It's actually really simple," Tristan declared, shifting on his crutches. "Look, I had no problem with Russell. Barely knew him. I'm sorry he's dead. But Hayden's still alive. He's the one you should be thinking of. We're his friends, and we have to help him."

Luke thought about when he'd asked Hayden to come pick up Tristan at the hospital. "Won't his . . . friends want to do that?" Hayden had replied. *He didn't give a shit about you,* Luke thought, looking up at Tristan's earnest, open face. *You're pathetic, really.*

"I know Hayden made a mistake," Tristan continued. "Look, when he drove Rachel's car into a tree, he messed up pretty bad. He's the reason my leg is so screwed up. But I know that he's a good guy, and he didn't mean to hurt anyone, and I forgive him."

So pathetic I can't even stand it. "Yeah, well . . ." Luke hoped Tristan would let it drop.

"I know they want you to testify," Tristan said.

"Yeah." Luke had been dodging Hayden's lawyer's calls for days. Hayden had left a message on Luke's cell phone the night before. Luke had just deleted it instinctively. He wasn't ready for something like that.

"Me too, you know," Tristan said. "I'm going to be a character witness."

"Cool."

"I didn't see you at the bail hearing," Tristan pointed out. "A few of us from the team went. To show support."

"I didn't go."

"Right," Tristan said, looking a little disgusted.

"I heard he didn't get bail," Luke attempted. "That sucks."

"You should talk to Hayden's lawyer," Tristan suggested.

"Yeah, I will," Luke conceded. "I guess that'd be a good idea." He stood up from the wall and started to head off. "Good luck with Dr. Locke."

CHAPTER 27

LUKE WAS READY to scream. He'd been sitting in his room for over an hour, trying to decide whether or not to go and talk to Hayden's lawyer. He knew he was probably going to have to go at some point, and that he probably wouldn't be able to put it off much longer. Plus, Tristan's words were still echoing through Luke's head. "Hayden's still alive," he had said. "He's the one you should be thinking of."

Luke's room was starting to suffocate him, and finally he stormed out and slammed the door behind him, turning his back on the *smack* the door made against the door frame. He walked outside, folding his arms and heading away from the dorm. He got about twelve yards away when he realized where he was going. He froze midstep, then changed direction, making a sharp left to head toward the athletic center, on the opposite side of campus from the cliff. He reached the building and circled around the side, rounding the corner and finding himself face-to-face with Cooper Albright. He thought about just walking away, but today he didn't feel like it.

Cooper was leaning casually against the wall, holding a joint between the fingers of his left hand. "Hey. It's you."

"Yep."

Cooper nodded, like Luke had said something particularly deep. "Heard about Applegate murdering that guy."

Luke felt his body tense. *You don't get to say that.* He took a step forward. "Murdering?" he repeated, not liking the way the word rolled off his tongue. "Is that what you just said to me?"

"Oh, am I wrong?" Cooper taunted. "Come on, tell me I'm wrong."

You don't get to talk about it like that.

"He killed him, right? You know he killed him. Or tell me I'm wrong."

"Fuck you."

"You can't, can you?"

"Holy shit," said Luke. "You are an *asshole.*"

"Okay," said Cooper. "Fine." He brought the joint to his lips and inhaled.

Luke took a second step forward. "You sold him coke." It was an accusation.

"What?"

"You sold him coke," Luke repeated.

"I sold a lot of people coke, Prescott. You're going to have to be more specific."

"You know who I mean," said Luke.

Cooper hesitated a minute, then said, "Yeah. So what?"

So that's why he crashed. That's why Tristan hurt his leg. That's why Russell had to join the team. That's why we were on the cliff. That's why.

Cooper shrugged. "It doesn't matter now. Doesn't matter what else we all did."

"It matters."

"Hayden Applegate did drugs," Cooper recited. "Hayden Applegate crashed a car. Hayden Applegate cheated on a test. Hayden Applegate beat up a freshman." He laughed. "None of it matters now. The only thing that matters now is that Hayden Applegate reached out with his hand and pushed Russell Conrad off a cliff. That's all there is now."

"'Hand,'" Luke repeated. *That's an awkward way of putting it.*

Cooper blinked. "What?"

"You said 'hand,'" Luke said slowly, processing. "Not 'hands,' 'hand.' How did you know Hayden only used one hand?"

"I—"

"I mean, I didn't even say that to the police."

Cooper's once-casual posture was now stiff, rigid. "Whatever, man."

"I didn't say anything because I didn't think it was important. So how did you know?"

Cooper shifted, cringing back against the wall. "What are you even . . . ? Why don't you get lost, huh?"

Luke stepped forward again, tilting his own head a little so that his eyes were almost level with Cooper's. "What did you see, Cooper?"

"Hey, I didn't see anything—"

"Bullshit."

"Prove it."

Luke jerked back, stunned. Cooper stared him down. They

stood there for a few minutes, locked in vicious eye contact. Finally, it was Luke who broke. It was Luke who gave in. He turned around slowly and took a few steps, half expecting Cooper to call out and stop him, to tell him what he knew. But Cooper didn't. And Luke walked away.

He went back into the dormitory. And he called Hayden's lawyer. And two days later, he walked into Hayden's lawyer's office, ready to talk.

CHAPTER 28

"ALL I WANT, Luke, is for you to tell the truth," said Martin Barnes, attorney-at-law. He was a heavyset man in his late fifties with a slight rasp to his voice and a neck that seemed to be just a few inches too short. He smiled when he spoke and did not instill in Luke the same sheer terror that the district attorney had. So far, talking to Martin Barnes had been almost easy. He'd seemed delighted that Luke was there, and he'd gone through quite a few pleasantries before circling around to the subject of their meeting.

"That's good," Luke said. "I'm going to tell the truth."

"Of course." The lawyer nodded. "Excellent. I just want to talk to you about what that truth is. For you." There was something funny about the way he said that, but Luke said nothing. "Why don't you tell me what happened that night?" said Mr. Barnes. "Can you do that?"

"Sure. Of course." Luke swallowed. "We went up on the cliff . . ." he said, realizing that this was the first time he'd told his story out loud since the night it happened.

"Russell went there with the intention of jumping, correct?" the lawyer asked, seeing Luke falter.

"Yeah." Luke swallowed again. "That's why we were all there. I think."

"You think?"

"That's why we were all there."

"Okay."

"And, um. And then Russell sort of chickened out." Was it wrong to say that about a dead person? Was it wrong even if it was true? "And so he and Hayden started arguing."

"About what?"

Luke thought back. He could hear their voices in his head, their words exactly. He could see them. Russell, grinning as he needled Hayden. Hayden, answering back in his dangerous, slippery voice. Hayden's hand flying out from his side. "Then *go!*" he'd yelled. The last words Russell ever heard.

"I don't want to talk about this anymore," Luke said, too loudly. He scrunched the skin on the back of his neck between his fingers.

Martin Barnes's face didn't change. "They are going for premeditated murder, Luke. Do you know what that means?"

"Yes," he responded thickly.

"Do you understand what would happen if Hayden were found guilty?"

"It would be bad," Luke answered.

"Yes," said the lawyer. "Very bad."

Luke nodded. He felt a lump in his throat, but he would not, not, not cry in front of this man. It was not going to happen. *I am eighteen years old,* Luke told himself, thinking that the number seemed much smaller than it usually did.

"There are three things we need to establish in your testimony," said Mr. Barnes. "First, that Hayden went up to the cliff with no intention of harming Russell. Second, that Russell antagonized Hayden into giving him a *light* push. Third, that the push alone was not the cause of Russell's fall, but Russell's own clumsy trip. How does that sound?"

"You don't need me to tell you my story," Luke muttered. "You've got it all figured out yourself."

Now the lawyer's face softened. "I'm sorry. I know this is difficult. But there is a lot at stake here right now. I want to make sure you understand that." His eyes searched Luke's face. "You are very important to this case, Luke. And I want to make sure that you understand that, too."

"I do."

"Okay," said the lawyer. "Because the prosecution is going to ask you a really important question. They're going to ask you if, as an eyewitness, you think Hayden was responsible for Russell's death. And if you want to help your friend, if you want to prevent very bad things from happening to him, you need to say no."

Luke exhaled. So this was what Angela Garvey had been getting at. This question. He looked at the lawyer, having the urge to plead with him for . . . something. "Hayden pushed him," he said, trying to explain. *This is why I can't tell you what you want to hear.*

But the lawyer didn't seem to understand. "One hand, two hands?" he asked, not missing a beat.

"Just with one hand."

"Lightly?"

"I'm not sure."

"But it could have been lightly?"

Luke squirmed in his seat. Things were getting flipped around, and he was forgetting what he meant. "I need to think."

"What do you need to think about, Luke?"

"I don't know."

"Okay." Mr. Barnes sighed. "Well, when we're done, you can go home and think. But for right now, you're going to talk me through what happened, exactly what transpired on that cliff. Then you do your thinking," he said. "You think about your friend. His future. I hope you think about that a lot."

CHAPTER 29

LUKE FOUND THEM on the quad, not that he was really looking for them. He was wandering around aimlessly, bored out of his mind because it was a Saturday and he had nothing to do. Drew and Freddy were passing a bottle conspicuously back and forth, and Courtney was stretched out on the grass in a bikini top, tanning. Another bikini-clad girl lay next to her. Luke approached, uncomfortably. They had been avoiding him. Or he had been avoiding them. By this point, he didn't know which.

"Hey." Courtney sat up. So did the other girl.

"Nicole!" Luke hadn't meant to sound so surprised. What was Nicole doing hanging out with them after they had been so awful to her about Russell? *So this is what it is. Hayden is gone, so back she comes.*

Nicole regarded him sternly behind dark sunglasses. "Hey, what's going on?" said Drew, pushing through the awkwardness in a flat voice.

It took Luke a moment to see it. The way they looked attentively at Drew when he talked. *How replaceable Hayden was . . .* The way Freddy lounged at Drew's elbow. *How replaceable I was . . .*

"Not a lot. Just hanging out." Luke tried to appear nonchalant.

"Yeah?" Drew did not invite him to sit. *Since when do I need an invitation?* Luke sat.

"Guess we haven't seen you around a lot," Freddy commented.

"Yeah. S'all just a little weird, you know." Something twisted in Luke's stomach. It was hard for him to be there with them, to be so out of place with them. It seemed like only hours ago that they were all scattered around a lunch table, talking about a fencing meet or an upcoming party. It used to be so easy. But of course, Hayden had been there. And Luke had been with Hayden. "Hayden being gone and all," Luke said, having been struck with the urge to remind them of their friend.

Nicole opened her mouth and then closed it, making a show of deciding not to say something.

"We didn't see you at Russell's memorial service," Freddy commented.

"Oh. Yeah. I figured that—"

"That it wouldn't be right," Courtney finished. But it hadn't been what Luke was going to say, and it jostled him a bit.

"We got trampled last week," said Freddy.

"What?"

"The meet," he clarified. "We put one of the guys from JV foil on saber with Alex and Ben. The squad didn't win a single bout."

Luke tried to care. When he and Hayden and Tristan had made up the saber squad, they had always come out with a winning record. "That sucks."

"We were strong in foil and épée, but it didn't make a difference," said Freddy.

"So why'd you walk out on us?" Drew spoke up. There was no missing the accusation.

Smarting, Luke pretended casualness. "Guess I didn't really feel like I was wanted."

Drew raised an eyebrow. "Team's a team."

What the fuck does that mean? "Yeah."

"So you're friends with Cooper Albright now?" said Courtney.

"Huh?"

She cocked her head to one side. "People just said."

"What people?" he demanded, then gave up. "No. I'm not friends with Cooper Albright."

"Yeah, he's friends with the purple-haired girl," said Freddy. There was a revolting little smile perched on the corner of his upper lip.

"Rachel. And I'm not friends with her either." *This is not going well.*

"My mistake," remarked Drew, though it had been Freddy who'd said it.

Luke cleared his throat. "So. Did you guys go to the bail hearing?" he asked, remembering what Tristan had said about people from the team going to show support for Hayden.

"Why would we?" Courtney sounded scandalized.

"I just thought . . ." Luke faltered. "I mean, Hayden—"

"Hayden *killed* someone," she interrupted, as Nicole stared dramatically away. "And if I were you . . ." She let the sentence hang, waiting for Luke to request that she complete it.

"If you were me?" Luke prompted tersely.

"If *I* were you," said Drew quietly, "I wouldn't make such a show of being Hayden's *buddy.*"

"Excuse me?"

Drew shrugged. "You and Hayden are the only ones who know what happened up there."

"And what, you think we pushed him off together?" Luke stood. "Fuck you."

Drew looked calmly up at him. "Maybe you should go."

CHAPTER 30

PER TRISTAN'S ADVICE, Luke had been avoiding Rachel since he'd been so mean to her in the room. He felt completely embarrassed by how he had acted. He was sure she hated him. He didn't know how he could face her. But one Friday afternoon, he was walking away from his last class of the day when he saw her walking toward him from the opposite direction. There was no way for him to go around her without being outwardly unkind, so he resigned himself to having to speak to her.

"Hey," he said with a nod.

For a second it looked to Luke like she would ignore him, and his stomach dropped. But finally she offered, "Hello."

They were standing on the small patio between the science center and the dining hall. It was a small stretch of bleached stone, with a few decorative benches and chairs that no one ever sat on. The school had obviously meant the patio to be a hangout place for students, but it was actually only used as a pathway.

"Nice day," said Luke.

"Yeah." She smiled shyly.

"How's it going?" he asked politely.

"Fine," she replied. "How're you?"

"I'm good," he lied. He clicked his tongue against the roof of his mouth, trying to figure out what to say to her. "You pierced your nose," he observed, noticing for the first time the gold stud that protruded from the top of her left nostril.

She blushed. "Yeah. Last week. Kind of a spur-of-the-moment thing. I'm not sure if I like it yet."

"It looks good."

"Yeah? Thanks." She hopped from foot to foot nervously. "Haven't seen you in a while."

"Everything's been nuts," he apologized.

"I thought maybe you were avoiding me," she joked.

Fuck it, might as well tell the truth. "I was, a little," he admitted.

"Oh." She looked crestfallen.

"But just because I thought you wouldn't want to talk to me!" he said quickly. "I mean, after I was such a jerk to you. I thought you'd be mad."

"I was never mad," Rachel protested. She paused. "Well, maybe for a little, but I get it. I mean, it was an awful night, and there I was the next morning pressing you to talk about it. I felt like such a bitch."

"No!" Luke was shocked. "You weren't a bitch at all. I was the bitch!"

Rachel giggled.

Luke's face turned red. "I mean, I was the jerk. Not you."

"Well, for what it's worth, I forgive you," she said. "I mean, if you can forgive me for being so insensitive."

"Let's forget it ever happened," Luke said, grinning at her. He was starting to feel pretty good.

Rachel laughed, tossing her purple hair over her shoulder. "Deal." Her face contorted into an expression of mock seriousness. "Should we shake on it?"

Luke played along. "Oh, most definitely. We should make it a binding contract." He stuck out his hand. She took it. Impulsively, he leaned in and quickly brought his lips up against hers.

Rachel pulled away. "Luke."

Luke stepped back, unsure of what he'd done wrong. "I'm sorry," he stammered. "I just thought . . ." *Too soon, too soon. Fuck! Too soon.*

"No, I'm sorry. It's just . . ." She tucked her hair jerkily behind her ear. "Tristan and I . . . Well, I just thought you hated me, and he and I have been friends for a really long time. I mean, he asked and . . ." Rachel stared down at the grass uncomfortably.

"You're going out with Tristan," Luke said dully.

"I'm sorry if I gave you the wrong idea." She looked up and met his eyes. "Really, Luke." She twisted her hands together. "I mean, it's been awhile since you and I even talked. And so I just . . . and, you know, I was mad at you. Ugh, I'm sorry."

Fuck. Luke took a deep breath and forced a smile. "It's okay. Really. I'm glad. I mean, about Tristan. He's pretty cool."

She looked relieved. "Can we still be friends?"

Oh, goody. "Yeah. Totally."

Rachel beamed at him. "So I was just about to get dinner. Come with me. We'll talk. As friends." Without waiting for a response, she started off toward the parking lot, and, glumly, Luke headed after her.

CHAPTER 31

LUKE BOUNCED HIS LEG up and down nervously in the blue-painted holding room. The metal chair pressed against his back, and small beads of perspiration formed on his brow. A loud buzz startled him, bringing his heart to his throat, as the door slid slowly open. A tall, dark-haired guard entered first, followed shortly after by Hayden, who was dressed in a blue jumpsuit that was nearly the same shade as the faded walls.

Hayden's face broke out into a broad grin when he saw Luke. He sat down in the chair across the table from Luke, and the guard said gruffly, "Just yell if you need anything." As soon as the guard left, Luke had the urge to run and bang on the door and demand that he be let out. *I don't belong here. I've changed my mind. I don't want to be here.* But no. It was time. He couldn't postpone it any longer. Avoiding Hayden wasn't helping anyone.

Maybe if Luke could just talk to him, things would start making more sense. Something would click, and then everything would seem easier. Hanging out with Hayden always made everything seem easier.

Once the guard was gone, Hayden visibly relaxed. "Luke, I'm so glad you're here."

"How are you?"

"I'm okay," Hayden answered. "I hate it here, though."

Well, it's jail, Hayden. You're not supposed to like it. "I'm sorry." There was a pause.

"Yeah, I was wondering if you were going to come." Hayden reddened. "I mean, I'm sure you were . . . busy and stuff."

Now it was Luke's turn to be embarrassed. "Yeah, I'm sorry. I meant to come sooner." *Three weeks. Three weeks I've left him here.*

"Yeah, I knew it," Hayden said, reassured. "I knew you were going to come. I just, well, you know." He shrugged. "This whole thing's making me a little crazy, I guess."

Luke's fingers rattled nervously on the cold, metal table. "I don't know. I guess I just had to, like, process or something. Yeah." He looked away, then back again.

"Oh." Hayden scratched his cheek. "So what's new? Tell me about something . . . else," he said.

"I quit the team," Luke offered.

Hayden blinked. "Why?"

"I don't know. It didn't seem that important anymore. I was getting tired of it, anyway. And the team's pretty much fucked since you and I and Tristan and Russell are all gone."

At the mention of Russell's name, Hayden stiffened, and Luke stopped talking. *Stupid. Why'd you have to bring it up? Stupid.*

They sat there in silence while Luke tried to recall all the conversation topics he'd carefully thought up during the train ride to the jail.

"So . . . my lawyer said you went to see him," Hayden said finally.

"Yeah, we had to talk about my testimony."

"Right, because you're the eyewitness." Silence again. "And . . ." Hayden shifted uncomfortably in his seat. "He also told me about that question." His eyes met Luke's. "The one the prosecution's probably going to ask you."

"Yeah." Suddenly, Luke wished the awkward silence would return. He flitted his eyes away, breaking contact.

"Luke, I mean, you're going to tell them it wasn't my fault, right?" Hayden said quickly, leaning forward in his chair. His blue eyes were wide, and he shoved back his dark hair in one quick jerk of his hand. "You were there. You saw what happened." He paused, breathing heavily. "You got my back on this, right?" he said softly, pleadingly.

And there it was, out in the open. Luke's throat went dry. "Yeah, I got your back." The words seemed to come out of his mouth without his control, and as soon as they had left him, he wished he could suck them back in. *How can I say that? It's a lie! I don't know what I'm going to do yet!*

Hayden's grin returned to his face. "I knew it. I knew you would." He let out his breath. "I mean, I thought for a second . . . Well, it doesn't matter." Hayden didn't seem to notice Luke's face, which was turning redder by the second. "You know, my lawyer, he wanted me to say that it was both of us. Said it might help my case. But I said no way, I got Luke's back because he's got mine, because we're like brothers."

Right. Not liking that lawyer so much anymore.

"Hey, Luke, you remember that time freshman year? When you and I played that trick on Mr. Mayer, with the toupee. And we put it up on the flagpole, do you remember?"

Okay, nostalgia. I guess now's as good a time as any. "I remember the three weeks of detention you got," Luke said, his voice unintentionally laced with admiration. The prank on their physics teacher had been masterminded by the fourteen-year-old Hayden. Luke, who had followed all the rules in junior high, had been impressed by Hayden's daring and had considered himself exceedingly lucky to have been included in the plot.

"You remember," said Hayden, "Mayer only caught me, but I didn't tell him you helped. I had your back."

Oh, shit. He's guilt-tripping me. Luke had to say something. "Look, Hayden, the thing is, I'm not exactly sure."

A pause. "What do you mean, you're not sure?" Hayden asked, his voice an octave too high.

"Well, it's just . . ." The words refused to come out. "Well, I mean, Russell's *dead.* I mean, you pushed him."

"Luke, you gotta—" Hayden swallowed. "I mean, you gotta help me here. I can't be in jail forever, Luke. You don't know what it's like here! I got a life. I mean, it wasn't my fault. You saw it. He tripped. I barely touched him." There was silence. Luke wanted to shrink into nothing. "Luke, you have to help me," Hayden said softly.

Luke stood, his cramped legs quivering slightly. He crossed the room shakily and knocked once on the door. The guard opened it immediately and asked, "You finished?"

Luke nodded. His skin icy cold, he walked slowly out of the room, leaving Hayden sitting there with his head propped up by one tired fist. Luke had nothing to say to him, nothing that would help, anyway. He was just as trapped as Hayden was now. He had no idea what to do. He wanted to just tell the truth, but he didn't know what it was.

Walking out of the jail, Luke could barely believe that this was how his life was ending up. *Here I am, visiting my best friend in jail.* It was surreal. And it was all so complicated.

Ironically, Luke had initially gone away to Briar Academy to get away from complication. Home life had been steadily deteriorating as his father had gotten more moody, more withdrawn. The night before he'd left, his parents had taken him out for a farewell dinner, just as they'd done for Jason the year before. It had been fun and mellow, and Luke had found himself wondering if he really needed to leave in the morning.

But the following day, he'd set off for Briar. Two days later, his father was dead. Luke always wondered if his father was just waiting until both his sons were out of the house. Or maybe that was just how the timing had worked out. Either way, it had been a hell of a going-away present.

CHAPTER 32

"YOU SHOULD COME BACK to practice," Tristan told Luke one afternoon when the two of them and Rachel were sprawled out on the grass between the English and science buildings. Tristan had just returned from his first fencing practice since the car accident.

"Yeah, I don't think I'm going to do that," Luke said, shrugging and watching the light glance off Rachel's purple hair.

She turned and frowned at him. "Why not?"

They were all lying on their stomachs, and Rachel had her arm resting across Tristan's back. Luke had been mainly hanging out with the two of them since he'd had that awful encounter with the four he now thought of as his former friends. For the most part, he enjoyed their company, though he would gladly do without the moments when they acted particularly couple-like. Luke wondered if Tristan knew about him and Rachel, what had almost been. He assumed not, since Tristan never seemed to show any jealousy or discomfort when he found them alone together, and he was always perfectly friendly toward Luke.

"I'm busy," Luke mumbled.

"Doing what?" she pressed.

"College stuff." This was not true. Luke had finished his second round of applications during winter break, and now he was just waiting to hear back from schools. In the meantime, he hadn't really been thinking about it. He was having trouble picturing a life that extended past his senior year of high school.

"Everyone misses you," Tristan said.

"Yeah?" Luke asked sharply. "Who's everyone?"

"Y-you know," he stammered. "Ben, Alex—everyone. The team."

Luke rolled his eyes. "Right. The same team that crosses to the other side of the hall when they see me? Yeah, they sure miss me."

"Luke . . ." Rachel said.

"You know the last time I saw Ben Sajjadi, he nearly knocked over a crowd of juniors trying to avoid me?" Luke asked, trying unsuccessfully to sound like he was kidding. His throat felt oddly stiff. "They're all like that now. Barely even look at me."

"They just don't know what to say to you," Tristan offered weakly.

"Yeah," Luke snorted.

"Give it time," said Tristan.

"Because in a couple of weeks they're going to want to be my friends again? Fuck that."

"You should just come back to practice," Tristan said. "People will stop being so freaked after a while."

"I'm not going back to practice." Luke hadn't known how sure he was until he said it. He would never go back to fencing. It was fencing that had gotten them up on that cliff. That stupid initiation process. It was fencing's fault.

"The team needs you," Tristan urged.

"I said I'm not going back," Luke said quietly, staring him down. "So back the fuck off."

"Don't you care about anyone but yourself?" Tristan blurted out.

Luke laughed through his teeth. "Right. Here we go."

"No way," Rachel said. "I'm sick of talking about this trial stuff. New topic. Please."

Tristan sighed. "It's kind of on our minds, Rach . . ."

"No," she said firmly. "I'm tired of listening to the two of you go back and forth over this. You don't agree. Fine. Just let it go."

"Let it go—?" he spluttered.

"I didn't say I don't agree," Luke interrupted. "I haven't decided yet what I'm going to do. All I'm saying is I'm still thinking about it."

She rolled her eyes. "Whatever."

"And what is there to think about, exactly?" Tristan asked Luke.

Rachel groaned. "Oh my God, don't."

"I'm just saying," he continued, putting up a hand toward Rachel defensively, "that this is really a pretty simple decision."

"Well, I don't see things as simply as you do, Tristan," Luke replied. "Jesus. You don't get it, do you?"

"Ugh, here we go again." Rachel shoved her forehead into the grass.

"What exactly am I supposed to be *getting?*" Tristan propped himself up on his forearms. "He's a good guy. He's in trouble. He needs help. That's what I *get.*"

"Okay, well, I don't need to say anything, do I?" Luke said disgustedly. "You already know everything."

Rachel lifted her head. "This is productive?" she asked. "What you're doing right now, this is useful to the two of you?"

"Let me just say this one thing," Tristan insisted.

"Haven't you said enough?" she snapped. "Luke's choice is his choice. Let's move on."

I think she's defending me. I think she's on my side. "Thank you."

She turned to him. "Oh, you shut up."

Maybe not.

"All I'm saying," Tristan said, making a show of shifting his back toward Rachel, "is that if I were in your place, I wouldn't have this much trouble with it. So that's what I don't understand." He shrugged. "I'm sorry."

"Well," Luke said quietly, "you weren't in my place. You weren't there. You didn't see Russell scream, you didn't see Russell fall, and you sure as hell didn't pull Russell's bloody corpse out of the lake."

Rachel's eyes widened. "Luke!"

Tristan glared at him. "I'm not saying what happened wasn't awful. I'm just saying that there's only one right thing left to do now."

"Is there? Is there even one?" Luke shot back.

"Oh, I'm done." Rachel stood. "I am so done."

Tristan leapt up. "Hey, I'm sorry. Wait."

"No," she said. "I've had it with both of you."

"Don't be mad," said Tristan. "We're sorry. Right, Luke?"

"Yeah," he muttered.

Rachel shrugged. "Whatever. I should go, anyway."

"I'll see you later?" Tristan asked, sounding worried.

"Yeah," she said brusquely, and stalked off, leaving Luke and Tristan on the grass, feeling like complete idiots.

That feeling was still with Luke the next morning, when he nervously approached Rachel at breakfast. She was sitting at their usual table; she and Tristan had been eating with him almost every day lately, though he wondered if that was mainly because they felt sorry for him. Luke stood self-consciously in front of her, holding his tray in front of him like a clumsy barrier. "Morning."

"Morning." She was chewing, so he couldn't tell if she was purposely refusing to smile at him. He sat down, and she didn't try to stop him. She swallowed. "I'm not mad at you."

"Okay," he said, a little thrown by her forthrightness.

She laughed. "Wow. That came out really awkward. Sorry."

His whole body relaxed. "Yeah. That did come out really awkward," he teased.

"Thanks. I try." She gulped down some orange juice. Luke liked that Rachel ate and drank like a real person: she didn't sip gracefully or take teeny little bites. Luke thought of Nicole and the way she would sometimes even cover her mouth with her hand while she chewed. It was ridiculous. Who was she trying to impress?

"Well, anyway, I'm glad you're not mad at me," Luke said.

"Yeah." Rachel looked sort of embarrassed. "And I'm sorry I walked off like that. Because I didn't want you to feel like I was just, like, abandoning you."

His heart sank. *Oh. Great. This is a pity thing.* "I didn't feel like that." She was making him feel like a complete loser. She flinched at his tone, though, so he quickly changed the subject. "Where's Tristan?"

"I don't know." She stuffed her mouth with eggs.

"You still mad at him?"

"Can't be mad at him and not you, can I?" Rachel said, which didn't really feel like an answer. She stared at Luke for a second. "You know, though, it's not really . . ." She hesitated. "He's just always egging you on and stuff."

"Yes!" Luke said, with inappropriate vehemence.

She didn't seem to notice. "Because this is obviously a really different situation for you than for him. And he just doesn't need to keep, like, perpetuating this same fight. Anyway, I tell him that, and he doesn't listen." She shrugged.

Luke sat up a little straighter, alert. "But you guys are okay, yeah?"

"What? Oh, yeah. Yeah, of course. We're fine." She stabbed a pancake sharply with her fork and brought it to her lips.

Oh well. "Good."

Rachel set down her fork. "It's just that sometimes he can be so completely frustrating."

Excellent.

"I feel like I say things, and he just ignores me. Because he's totally positive he's right. So he just doesn't take anything in. And I can't feel justified getting mad at him, because he doesn't do it in a mean way or anything. He's the nicest . . . ignoring person . . . ever."

"Like passive-aggressive," Luke offered.

She frowned. "Not really."

"Oh."

"You know what it is? It's kind of like everything's so straightforward with him. And you tell him something different and he doesn't even hear it, because he's already so sure. He doesn't . . . stress over things or get indecisive or whatever. He's just always so sure."

"I'm jealous," Luke said honestly.

"Ugh, but it's so annoying." Rachel groaned, then cracked up. "Listen to me. I've got a nice, confident boyfriend, and that's what I'm complaining about."

"No, you should complain," Luke said. "I mean, I totally understand what you're saying. Absolutely." *Not at all. But keep trashing Tristan.*

She nodded. "Well, thank you for saying that. Because sometimes I think I'm going crazy. I mean, isn't it supposed to be a good thing that he's always got such a clear idea of what's right? Isn't that what makes him such a solid guy?"

"But it pisses you off," Luke prompted.

"Yeah. Yeah, it pisses me off." She shook her head. "Sometimes—this is going to sound really horrible—"

Say it. Say it.

"Sometimes I just feel like he's totally unoriginal."

I have no idea what that means.

There was a pause, and her eyes widened. "You can't tell him I said that, Luke." She spoke with sudden urgency. "I probably shouldn't have said that. It's on my mind, that's all, because I'm a little annoyed still."

Am I original?

"Luke? Are you listening?"

"Yeah? What? No, I wouldn't say anything." He meant that. It was important to him that Rachel trusted him.

She grimaced. "You should really forget I said any of this stuff."

What counts as original? "Consider it already forgotten." *I'm probably original.*

"Good." She smiled. "I'm glad we can talk about things like this." She brushed a lock of hair behind her ear. "And I'm glad we're friends. It's good to have someone to vent to."

Luke grinned gallantly. "Any time." *Girls don't stay with unoriginal boyfriends, do they? They dump them, probably. And then they go out with other guys.*

"And I'm sure Tristan and I will work this out."

"I'm sure you will." *This turned out to be a very good morning after all.*

"I'm just in a bad mood, that's all."

Luke frowned sympathetically, but inside he was beaming. Maybe Tristan and Rachel would break up. Maybe they would break up soon.

CHAPTER 33

HEADMASTER GRUNBERG called Luke into his office several times over the next few weeks. He seemed to be trying very hard to get Luke to talk to him about what had happened, but Luke flatly refused. The headmaster had also attempted to speak to him about his grades, which had dropped, and his social circle, which had dwindled. Each time Luke tried to feed him the answers he wanted to hear—that he was having a tough time but he felt better every day and expected things would get back to normal very soon. And although the headmaster often seemed unsatisfied with these conversations, Luke never expected the phone call that the old man would make, and he never expected that one day he would be called to the headmaster's office and find that Grunberg was not alone.

The old man was seated behind his desk, and Luke's mother sat in one of the two chairs in front of it. Both turned to look at him when he entered. There was silence. Then Headmaster Grunberg said, "I'll give you two some time," and left.

Luke stared uncomprehendingly at his mother. *What is she doing here?*

She sighed, folded one spindly leg over the other, and adjusted the gray skirt of her business suit. "All right," she said, her clipped voice breaking the silence. "What now?"

"What?"

Her papery skin tightened visibly over her collarbone. "Well, I'm just trying to figure out what you want, Luke."

"I . . ." He didn't understand.

"Do you want to leave school? Is that what this is? You don't want to graduate?"

"What are you talking about?" Luke sputtered, bracing himself against the onslaught of his mother's hostility.

"I'm talking about the phone call I get from the head of your school telling me that I have to come down here because you can't seem to get your act together," she said. "I'm talking about your new D+ average, and the fact that you quit your fencing team. I'm talking about how you've got everyone concerned because you're ignoring all of your friends."

"I am not ignoring them; they're—"

"And I'm just *assuming* you didn't get into Dartmouth in December since you didn't even have the decency to *tell* me."

"Well, I really didn't think you cared," Luke snapped.

"I do care, Luke. But I'm tired. I'm tired of trying to show you that *constantly*, feeling like I've got something to *prove* to you." She laughed unsettlingly. "You make everything so hard, you know that? So I'm tired. I'm done."

"So that's why you're here? To tell me you're done?" He smirked. "You could have sent a text."

"What do you want?" she asked. "Why don't you *ever* tell me what you want?" It only made him angrier.

"You never cared what I wanted before!" he accused. "You never, ever cared!"

Her whole body cringed. "That is not true. Don't rewrite history. We went through a hard time there, and I . . . didn't do the things I should have, but you shouldn't say that . . ." She faltered. "I am so tired, Luke."

You don't get to be tired.

"Okay." Her voice got very quiet. "Well, you can hate me forever—that is your choice—but you should know that, for me, it ends here. I'm done."

You're always done. He laughed, a short bark of frustration. "Yeah. Great. Well, like I said, I don't want anything. So you can go." He meant to sound strong, defiant, but something went wrong with his voice at the end. It cracked, and he sounded so very young.

His mother's face softened. "I know that you've had a difficult year—"

That was the last straw. "You don't know anything," he hissed. "Don't tell me you know. You don't know because you don't want to know. You don't want to hear about anything that doesn't fit into your perfect little fantasy world. And that's why nobody wants to be around you. That's why Dad didn't want to be around you." There was a pause. *Wait. Maybe that was too much. Wait. Wait.*

His mother didn't flinch. "I'm surprised it took you so many years to say that."

"I didn't mean it." *Wait.*

"Of course you did," she said, so quietly. She stood, smoothing the front of her skirt with her palms. She looked unbearably tired. "I think I should go."

He hadn't wanted her there in the first place, but he didn't like the idea of her walking out on him. He also didn't like the exhausted expression etched across her face. "I didn't mean to say it was your fault," he said, not fully understanding why he was suddenly so upset. "I'm sorry."

"No. No, you said what you meant."

"Mom."

"Don't act like you care, Luke. We both know you don't."

He said nothing. She stared at him a moment, in a way she never had before. Then she turned, slowly, and left him there. He wanted to call after her, but he wasn't sure what he'd say.

CHAPTER 34

MARCH FADED into April. Hayden's court date was set for the middle of the month, and to Luke's disappointment, Tristan and Rachel did not break up. They seemed pretty united when they showed up at Luke's dorm room on Briar Academy's movie night. Luke had not planned on going to movie night. Last year he had gone with his old group of friends, and they'd sat in the back, laughing and talking through most of *X-Men*. This year it wouldn't be like that. Everyone would stare at him, and there would be whispers, and it would be awful. He wasn't going.

"Except you have to," Rachel informed him when she and Tristan refused to be turned away. "Because we are instituting a no-moping rule."

"I do not mope," Luke protested.

"Luke," Tristan said, smiling. "There is no way we are going to leave you here to sulk all night."

Luke knew that Tristan was, as always, just trying to be kind, but he couldn't help hating him just a little. *I'm not some little project for the two of you. It's embarrassing.* "I'm tired," he said. "I don't really feel like it."

"You know," Rachel said, "you can't expect people to . . . re-adjust to you if you don't let them." She winced. "That's a bad way of putting it."

"What she means," Tristan translated, "is that if you want people to start acting like they're comfortable around you, you can't spend all your time hiding out in here."

Luke glared at him. "I don't hide out."

"Don't get mad," said Tristan. "It's only some advice. All we're trying to say is that you have friends out there, plenty of them, who'd be there for you if you'd just put yourself out there a little more."

"Sure. Whatever." *Stop being so nice to me. I would never be this nice to you.*

"No, I'm serious," Tristan pressed. "Come with us tonight, have some fun, and show everybody they don't need to be afraid of you or nervous around you."

"And what if I don't care about how they feel?" Luke asked. "Did it ever occur to you that maybe I don't *want* my old friends back?"

"You don't mean that," Tristan said.

"Actually," Rachel said thoughtfully, "his old friends are pretty horrible."

Tristan rolled his eyes. "Okay, ignore her. The point we're trying to make—"

"No, look, I get it," Luke said. "But I'm just not going to waste my time trying to win over the people who . . ." He didn't know how to finish that sentence without sounding like a baby.

"They just didn't know how to talk to you," Tristan said.

"And it doesn't help that you stalk around like a freaking zombie all the time," Rachel put in helpfully.

Tristan shot her a look. "What we mean, Luke, is that maybe if you want to get things back to normal, you sort of have to make the first move."

"We're not trying to tell you what to do." Rachel paused. "Well, actually, we are, but we're right, so you should listen to us." She grinned. "Besides . . ." she said brightly, reaching into her backpack and pulling out a bottle of rum, "we brought refreshments!"

Luke considered the bottle. Getting drunk out of his mind suddenly seemed a lot more appealing than staying home sober. He looked at Rachel's and Tristan's eager faces. *They're not going to drop this. Might as well just go and get trashed.* "Ugh, fine. Let's go."

The movie was being shown in the dining hall. A screen had been unrolled on the far wall, and students were already crowded around tables pushed up near the front of the room. Luke, Tristan, and Rachel grabbed a table near the back and settled in. Across the room, Luke could see Drew, Freddy, Courtney, and Nicole watching him from their table. He tried to ignore them, but he could see them whispering and he knew they were talking about him.

"How long until it starts?" Luke asked, wishing the lights would go down.

Tristan checked his watch. "Couple minutes."

"And it wouldn't kill you to smile a little," Rachel suggested.

Luke's eyes flitted back to the table of his old friends. *I should not have come here.* He stood. "I'm going to get a drink."

"We *have* stuff to drink," she said.

"I know. Um, water." He made a beeline for the drinking fountain just outside the dining hall. He didn't take a drink. He just gripped the metal sides with both hands and leaned over the basin.

"Luke?" He turned. Standing a few feet away was Nicole Johnston. She gave him a weird sort of half smile and approached. "Hey. I thought I saw you over there."

Did she follow me out here? Why would she do that?

"Been a while." She bobbed her head up and down once. "How are you?"

I know you don't care how I am. You're forgetting how well I know you. What do you want?

When he didn't answer, Nicole's face flushed a little. "I was just thinking . . . I mean, we haven't hung out in ages."

He tried to keep his voice casual. "I've been around." He remembered the last time he'd spoken to her, when Drew had told him to get away from them and Nicole had just sat there. What was she doing coming over to him now and acting like that hadn't happened?

"Things are kind of weird with you and Drew, huh?"

Things are kind of weird with me and all of you. "Yeah."

"Well, I just wanted to check in," she said. "You know, see how you're doing."

Bullshit. "Have you gone to see Hayden yet?" Luke asked, to shock her a little.

It worked, and she was quiet for a few seconds. "Are you mad at me, Luke?"

The question struck him as tremendously funny. "Yeah, Nicole. A teeny bit."

Her eyes narrowed. "Well, you shouldn't be. And it's pretty immature of you. I never made anyone do anything."

"I hope that helps you sleep," Luke retorted.

"You shouldn't say that," she said. "It's awful of you to say that." She looked down. "You can't make anyone murder anybody," she told the floor. "It doesn't work like that."

"It wasn't murder!" Luke blurted out, unsure if he believed himself.

Her head snapped up. "How can you say that? Russell is *dead.*"

Luke scrambled to find words. "I'm just saying we don't know what exactly . . ." *What do I mean?* "Russell was—"

"Don't you *dare,*" she interrupted him, her eyes wild. "Don't you *dare* say anything bad about Russell! He was kind and sensitive and compassionate, and he was ten times better than you or Hayden or anyone, so just don't you *dare.*"

Kind? Sensitive? Compassionate? Russell? "I don't care," he told her. "I don't care if he was fucking Gandhi."

She swallowed, looking at him with obvious hatred. But when she spoke, her voice was very controlled. "Well, it isn't about Russell right now. Right now it's about Hayden."

"Fine. Great. I don't care."

"Hayden should pay for what he did," Nicole said, moving even closer to Luke. "His life should end like Russell's ended. You know it's what's right."

It hit him then. This was why she was talking to him. This was what it was all about. She knew he was going to testify, and she'd come over to convince him to incriminate Hayden on the stand. "Get away from me."

"Do you really think he should walk away from this?" she asked. "He should be able to just get on with his life like nothing ever happened?" She shook her head. "It's bad enough that you get to."

"What is that supposed to mean?"

"You know exactly what I mean. Who knows what you really did that night? Or what you didn't do that you could've? But nobody's going to make you pay for this. *He* at least should have to."

"I said, get away from me!" he shouted into her face.

She stiffened and stepped back. "You know it's what's right," she repeated as she walked away.

What you didn't do that you could've. Her words echoed through his head. *I didn't do a lot of things.* He swallowed hard. *But maybe I couldn't have stopped it anyway. Maybe it was just going to happen. And if not, well, what good does it do to dwell on this now?* He glared after Nicole, hating her for making him think about these things.

Luke waited in the hallway, calming himself down, until he saw the lights go down in the dining hall. Then he slunk in and took his seat next to a relieved-looking Rachel. As soon as the opening credits began to roll, Tristan pulled out the glass bottle. There were no chaperones nearby, so Tristan made no effort to hide the rum. Luke snatched the bottle from Tristan and took a long drink.

"Wow, save some for us, huh?" Rachel took the bottle from Luke's hand and, giggling, tilted the bottle's nose downward and let the liquid stream into her mouth. A small trail of rum trickled down her chin and onto her white T-shirt. "Oops. My bad."

"Still learning how to drink without spilling?" Tristan teased, taking the bottle from her. As he drank, he draped an arm around her shoulders, and she curled into him, planting a kiss on his cheek. Luke felt nauseous.

On the screen, Keanu Reeves was dangling down an elevator shaft as people in the elevator screamed frantically for help. The tension and suspense of the movie were rising. It didn't matter to Luke. What mattered was the steady warmth that was slowly spreading through his body.

They sat watching the movie for half an hour, passing the bottle among the three of them. Luke could feel himself getting drunker and drunker, and he welcomed the feeling, taking larger gulps of rum than Tristan or Rachel each time the bottle came around to him.

A sudden movement on Luke's left, and Drew Devonshire was sliding casually into the seat next to him. Without asking, Drew eased the bottle across the table from Tristan's fumbling fingers. Drew brought it to his lips and took a long drink as Tristan blinked glassily, trying to figure out how it was that the bottle had jumped from his hands to Drew's.

"Take it all, why doncha?" Luke slurred angrily at Drew. A voice in the back of his head told him Drew had only come over to mess with him and that he should just ignore him, but Luke pushed that voice away.

"Lighten up," said Drew. "We're just sharing."

"Shut up!" someone yelled.

"Get your own drink," Luke mumbled. His lips felt heavy, and he couldn't move them properly.

"Go to hell," Drew replied. He smiled.

That really pissed off Luke. Who did Drew think he was? "Don't tell me what to . . ." Finishing the sentence suddenly seemed overwhelmingly difficult to Luke. He could *show* Drew what he meant. Luke stood up clumsily, causing the bottle to fall to the ground and shatter.

"Now look what you've done, you moron." Drew's voice was loud, and the angry shouts of "Shut up, we're trying to watch the movie!" were ignored.

"Yeah? Yeah?" Luke took a swing at Drew with his right fist. His balance not quite right, he fell forward. Drew dodged easily and shoved his fist into Luke's stomach. Luke felt the wind get knocked out of him and kicked outward with his left foot, catching Drew in the shin. Drew swore, and Luke felt hands on his shoulders, pulling him back.

No one was listening to the movie anymore. No one cared that a bus was going to explode if Keanu didn't catch a psychotic killer. All eyes were on Drew and Luke. The shouts of "Shut up!" disappeared. This was way more exciting than the movie.

"Tell me something, Luke." Drew started to laugh. "What does it feel like to be best friends with a cold-blooded killer? What's that like? To be best friends with a *murderer?*"

Luke lunged forward again, and this time the hands holding him couldn't hang on. Or didn't want to anymore. Luke swung his fist forward and upward blindly, not caring now. And then, as he looked into Drew's eyes, just before fist connected with nose, Drew's face *changed.* Suddenly, it was Hayden's face staring back at him. Luke smashed his fist into it.

CHAPTER 35

LUKE HAD BEEN REALLY drunk only twice before in his life. The most recent time was a year or so ago at a team dinner, when Ward McAfee had managed to get his hands on a keg. Hayden had said he wanted to teach Luke how to do a keg stand, and Luke remembered hanging upside down above the keg with Freddy and Hayden each holding one of his legs. He also remembered the morning after, when he'd sworn he'd never get that drunk ever again. The time before that had been the night he'd found out his father was dead, and Hayden had insisted that the best remedy for grief was to get completely wasted. Luke remembered that hangover, too. It had been much worse than the second.

He woke up the morning after movie night with a hangover that was somewhere in between the two. His head ached, and his last memory was a shady vision of his fist slamming into someone's face. Hayden's. No, that wasn't possible. Hayden was in jail until his trial. Drew. Yes, that was whose face he'd punched. Punched. Drew. He jumped off his bed with a start, and he instantly regretted it. Pain was pulsing through his brain, bouncing off the insides of his temples, and ricocheting below his eyeballs. He was fully dressed in his clothes from the night before.

A knock smashed the air, and Luke reeled around. Rachel stood in the doorway, a shy smile on her face and a steaming beverage in her hand. She didn't look hungover at all. In fact, to Luke, she looked perfect. "Hey, how are you feeling?" she asked him. Luke groaned truthfully, and Rachel laughed, entering. She shoved the cardboard cup into Luke's hand. "Coffee," she said. "Black. It'll help with the"—she winked—"Irish flu."

Luke brought it to his lips and took a sip. "What happened last night?"

"Before or after you beat the crap out of Drew Devonshire?" Rachel asked innocently, sitting herself down at the end of Hayden's bed.

Luke sat down next to her. "Is he okay?"

"You're not getting kicked out, if that's what you're asking. Drew can't talk without admitting he was drinking."

Luke felt like he ought to be relieved, but the feeling was buried under waves of nausea. He swallowed hard. "How'd I get home last night?"

"Tristan and I brought you back. Had to sneak you past half the faculty on the way here."

"I owe you." The last thing he needed was to wind up in front of Headmaster Grunberg in the middle of all this mess. That might have sent him back into Dr. Locke's office.

"Don't worry about it."

Luke stared into her eyes. "I mean it. Thank you."

He was unsure if it was just his imagination, but it seemed to

Luke as if Rachel leaned in toward him. Neither said a word as their faces stood inches apart. Then the moment passed, and Rachel stood up briskly. "Well, you're lucky it's a Saturday. So take it easy today, okay?" she said, heading for the door.

Luke recovered quickly. "Yeah. I'll see you later."

"*Adiós.*" Rachel left, shutting the door gently with a sound that seemed to Luke as if it would shatter the glass of the room's windows.

He groaned and lay back down on the bed. He felt like he should get up, take a shower, get dressed. But then . . . *ow!*

I punched Drew. The words seemed so absurd to him, that he, Luke Prescott, would actually *hit* somebody. Luke remembered being in the sixth grade and seeing his older brother come home one day with a split lip and a two-day suspension. Jason had tried to explain about his opponent, an eighth grader who was selling pot to the fifth graders. Luke's father wouldn't listen. "It has taken the civilized world centuries to overcome the necessity for the use of brute force to solve problems, and no son of mine will bring about its return," he had said.

Luke had been listening from up on a staircase when Jason and his father had been arguing, and while their father's words seemed to have no effect on Jason, who would receive many more suspensions for fighting over the years, Luke had taken the words to heart.

But Luke had never been violent, not even as a little kid. He'd been shy, the one always in a corner. Even in elementary school, he was more likely to be found reading under a tree than out playing foursquare with his classmates. Luke had always been a loner. That was how it was, up until high school, when he'd met Hayden. Luke had become a part of Hayden's world, where things would always sort themselves out on their own, no effort required. A world that seemed to have vanished in an instant.

That world was locked up with Hayden in a jail cell. Because Hayden had killed Russell. The thought made Luke's head hurt even more. All the times that Hayden and Luke had sat up in their room, saying bitterly how some days they wished that a huge anvil would just fall on Russell's head, suddenly seemed sick and twisted and abnormal. But even then, it was just talk. They'd never wanted it to happen. At least Luke hadn't.

The more times Luke played the scene on the cliff over in his head, the more it seemed like a bad made-for-TV movie. How could Hayden, in his right mind, kill someone?

Luke frowned. But what if Hayden hadn't been in his right mind? What if Hayden had been on something? It explained everything. He would go talk to Hayden the next day. Hayden would tell him the truth, that he'd taken something from Cooper beforehand, or that he'd drunk something earlier that night. It would all make sense.

Luke could forgive Hayden for that. He could forgive Hayden for killing Russell as long as Hayden hadn't been in control when it had happened. For the first time in a while, lying on his back in the room, the world spinning around him and his head pounding, Luke really smiled. After he talked to Hayden, it would all be okay.

CHAPTER 36

THE PALE BLUE ROOM was just the same as it had been before. The paint on the walls was no less chipped, the cold metal chair no less uncomfortable, the look in Hayden's eyes no less haunting. Luke felt queasy. Hayden was stuck here in this never-changing vortex, this time freeze.

"Hey," Luke started tentatively. "How're you doing?"

Hayden shrugged. "I'm all right. Got moved up to minimum security. Good behavior."

"That's great," Luke said, his voice forced.

Hayden leaned back in his chair, and for a moment he looked the same as a few months ago, in the back row of Mr. Mehta's Latin class, relaxed and casual, probably planning the best way to get out of the detention that would inevitably be assigned to him before the period was over. But that was then and this was now.

"Couple guys from the team came by yesterday," Hayden offered.

"Yeah?"

"Said you slugged Drew Devonshire the other night. Did you really?"

"I was drunk," Luke said, embarrassed, as if that was an excuse. He felt the tips of his ears slowly becoming hot.

"Hey, well, no complaints here," said Hayden.

Luke shifted his body in the metal chair. "I guess you know, then . . ."

"What all my good friends are saying about me? Yeah, I know. It's just a few guys who come to visit me, so I figured." Hayden suddenly reddened. "Anyway, fuck them. We knew they were idiots, didn't we?"

"I don't hang out with them anymore," Luke said, feeling like he had to explain himself. "Even before the thing with Drew. I mean, when I hit him."

"Yeah, it's about time you found your backbone, Jelly," Hayden teased.

A smile flickered on Luke's face. It had been an inside joke between the two of them. Jelly, as in jellyfish, as in a spineless creature made of gelatin that just floated through life, going with the tides, the ebb and flow of the ocean. Hayden had always made fun of Luke, saying he had to stand up for himself. That he had no spine, no backbone. It had been funny then, and somehow, possibly because of the setting, it was funny now.

Luke started to feel sick. This wasn't right. They were laughing and joking in this room, as if nothing had happened. As if there wasn't a real reason they were here. As if Hayden wasn't in jail. As if Russell wasn't decaying six feet under. "I gotta ask you something, Hayden. It's important."

Hayden's grin faded. "Okay. Shoot."

"That night on the cliff—"

"Damn it, Luke!" Hayden's voice shot out through clenched teeth. His tongue smacked hard against his teeth, and Luke jumped. "Do we really have to talk about that?" Hayden caught sight of Luke's shocked face and softened. "Look, Luke, it's just . . . well, I mean, I just . . ." His voice faded into the walls.

"I just want to know, Hayden," Luke said carefully, and when Hayden didn't stop him he kept going, as cautiously as if he were walking on shards of glass, "if that night, when you did what you did, were you . . . ?"

"What?" Hayden asked sincerely. He really didn't know what Luke was trying to say. Hearing himself, Luke didn't blame him.

Don't make me say it. "Well, were you, you know . . . ?"

"No, what?"

"Were you, that night, I mean . . . were you . . . ?" His arm made a desperate gesture across the table. *Come on.*

"What are you asking me?" Hayden frowned, confused.

Crap, here goes. "Were you on something? Like the night of the car crash. I mean, were you high?" *Please, please, please, please, please.*

Hayden let out his breath in a sigh, a real sigh, like the air from his lungs was just pouring out of his broken body. "God, Luke, I wish I could say that I was."

No, no, no, no, no. "Are you sure?" *Say you forgot, but you were drunk or high. Say you were stoned. Say you took something from Cooper. Say your head was messed up. I'll believe you.*

"Yeah, Luke. I'm sure. I wasn't on anything. I—" Hayden's voice broke, and he swallowed. "It was me. No drugs."

Luke closed his eyes, his last hope dashed. He opened them

again, saw the look in Hayden's eyes as they drilled into him. *It's not fair.*

"No, I guess not," Hayden said quietly, and Luke realized that he'd spoken aloud.

He met Hayden's eyes. "We can't go back."

"No. We can't." Hayden's voice was barely audible, as if he was willing to say the words but didn't want to hear them himself.

And Luke looked at Hayden, really looked at him for the first time since that night on the cliff. And what he saw terrified him. There was something in Hayden's eyes, behind the childlike fear. There was something colder.

His face, with the chiseled features that Luke had once envied, had hardened as well. The boyish roundness had been steadily chipped away to leave only a solid, set, almost angry face, a small stubble of brown hair lining his chin and the sides of his face. He looked different. He looked older. This wasn't the Hayden Applegate that Luke knew. This impostor, sitting there in that metal chair, in the jumpsuit with the black number on the breast pocket, barely even *looked* like Hayden.

Luke stood, and Hayden made no move to do the same. "I wish we could. Go back, I mean," Luke said.

"Me too," Hayden said softly.

There was no sympathy in Luke's voice as he said goodbye. It was way too late for sympathy. There were decisions that had been made. Whether they'd been premeditated or spur of the moment, they'd still been made. And consequences came with those decisions.

CHAPTER 37

"SO I'M ASSUMING you've had some time to think since our last meeting." Luke was back in the district attorney's office. Angela Garvey had wanted to speak to him once more before the trial.

"Um, yeah." It was true. He had been thinking. He just hadn't really come up with anything yet.

"And I understand you're being called as a witness for the defense."

"Yeah." He'd gotten the letter a week ago, a small note from the defense attorney saying: "We know we can count on you."

Angela Garvey leaned her pretty, sharklike face across her desk. "So I guess what I'm wondering is, what does Martin Barnes know that I don't?"

"Uh. I mean, I said I was going to say what I saw, so . . ."

"And what exactly was that?"

"Hayden, um, pushing him and, um, him falling."

"And that Hayden's pushing him caused him to fall," she prompted.

"I don't know."

She sighed, reminding him unpleasantly of his mother. "Obviously you want to help your friend. So don't you think, if that were the right thing to do, this would be a whole lot easier for you?"

"I . . ."

"The fact that you're having such a hard time shows that you do know what's right. And it's not helping Hayden Applegate beat a murder charge."

Luke was quiet. In a weird way, she was making sense to him.

"Luke," she said in a softer tone of voice. "I'm sure that Hayden is a good friend. I'm sure that you care about him. But someone died because of his actions. Actions that I think you know he meant to carry out. And that is way bigger than friendship."

Luke pressed his palm as hard as he could into the back of his neck. "I don't know."

"Yes, you do," said the district attorney. "So at trial, when I ask you if Hayden was responsible for Russell's death, I want you to tell me what you know to be true. Can you do that?"

But I still don't know what's true. "I'll say what I saw," Luke answered. The district attorney smiled and said, "Good," and Luke left her office feeling like he'd lied to her.

The days went by, and soon there was less than a week until the Trial. Luke had started thinking of it like that, with a capital letter. He couldn't get it out of his head. He couldn't make himself forget about it even for a second. It was set to begin on Wednesday, and by early Monday the pressure of too many questions had taken its toll on Luke. He hadn't been able to really sleep for the past few days, and he was exhausted. His brain just couldn't focus on anything. He needed to talk to someone, but he didn't know who. He obviously couldn't talk to his mother. He didn't want to dump all of this mess onto Rachel. He already knew exactly how Tristan felt about what he should do.

Maybe he could call Jason. Luke figured Jason wouldn't be all that much help, but it would still be good to be able to vent a little. Besides, Luke reminded himself, he hadn't spoken to Jason in a while, not since they'd both been in Springfield. It would be good to talk to his brother.

He picked up his cell phone and dialed Jason's, realizing that he wasn't even sure where his brother was living now. It had been so long since they'd spoken.

Jason picked up on the sixth ring. "Hello?" The voice sounded sleepy.

"Jason?"

"Who the hell is this?"

Oh, right. It's three thirty in the morning. People aren't so perky at three thirty in the morning. "Jason, it's Luke."

"Luke?"

"Yeah."

"You calling from school?"

"Yeah." *Where the hell else would I be?*

"Something wrong?"

"No." *Yeah.* "Yeah. Yeah, something's wrong."

Luke could hear Jason stifle a yawn on the other end of the phone. "Okay, Luke, what's up?"

Suddenly, Luke realized he had no idea how to explain it. "Well, it's kind of complicated."

"Is this about what happened with that friend of yours?

Hayden? Mom told me about the whole thing on that cliff with that kid who died. Is that what this is about?"

"Yeah."

"I was gonna call you. When that happened. But I've been doing stuff and . . ." Jason trailed off. "I should have called you. I'm sorry. I should have."

"It's okay." *It is not okay.*

"Are you all right?"

"I need to talk to you."

"Now?" Jason yawned loudly.

"Um . . ."

"I mean, can't this wait?"

"Not really."

Jason sighed and the phone crackled. "Okay. So talk to me."

It all came out at once. What had happened on the cliff, how Russell had died, how Hayden had gotten hauled off to jail, the meetings with the lawyers. "And now I've got no fucking idea what to do," Luke finished, realizing he'd been swearing a lot more lately.

There was a pause. Luke waited. "Jesus, Luke, that sucks."

I called my brother and spilled my guts so I could hear that?

"Luke, we really should talk."

Aren't we talking now?

"But, when I'm awake. You know, face-to-face," Jason said.

"Where are you?"

"Springfield. I'm staying with Mom."

Still? "Oh."

"I'll drive down on Tuesday. I'll meet you at the Grill, okay? We'll get burgers or something and talk. At, like, six?"

Luke was overwhelmed with gratitude. "Yeah! Yeah, thanks. Thanks a lot."

"Don't mention it," Jason mumbled, yawning again. "Okay. I'll see you then."

"Okay." Luke started to pull away from the phone.

"Oh, and Luke?"

Luke brought the phone back to his ear. "Yeah?"

"You ever call me this late again and I'll kill you."

And a dial tone rang in Luke's ear. Luke snapped the phone shut and climbed back into his bed. Jason was coming. His brother was coming, and he would tell him what to do.

CHAPTER 38

LUKE TRIED TO FOCUS during his classes on Monday, but he was too tired and drained to do anything but stare blankly down at his desk. He wondered if he was failing. He wondered if it mattered.

Coming out of his last class, physics, Luke ducked into a side stairwell of the science building to avoid Courtney Chase, whom he saw walking down the hallway in his direction. The stairwell was empty, white, and sterile-looking. Luke took a few steps forward, and his sneakers skidded slightly. The floor had just been cleaned and was still damp. Luke thought back.

A few weeks into their first year at Briar, fourteen-year-old Luke and Hayden had snuck into this stairwell in the middle of the night. It'd been raining outside, and Luke's sneakers had skidded on the stairs. He'd fallen, slammed his shoulder into the wall, and yelled out. Hayden froze and put his fingers to his lips. "Shh! They'll hear us!" he whispered.

Luke nodded and pulled himself to his feet. "Sorry."

It had been Hayden's idea to come in the first place. He had heard there was a telescope, used only for the astronomy classes, on the locked fourth floor of the science building. "I want to see it," he'd told Luke.

"Why?"

He'd grinned. "Because it's *locked.*"

But Luke didn't really want to be there. The building was a little creepy at night, and Luke certainly didn't feel comfortable enough at Briar Academy to be breaking its rules. "Maybe they already heard us," he said. "Maybe we should head back. Try again some other time."

Hayden rolled his eyes. "Come on," he said, and started off up the stairs. Luke trailed behind. They reached the top of the stairwell and stopped in front of a thick, sturdy-looking door. Hayden tried the handle, confirming that it was, in fact, locked.

"Okay," Luke said. "Now what?"

"Don't worry," replied Hayden. "I came prepared." He pulled a credit card out of his pocket.

Luke eyed it skeptically. "You're going to buy your way in?"

"No, dumbfuck. I'm going to use it to open the door." Hayden jammed the card into the space between the door and frame. "I think I just stick it in here and . . ." He wiggled it around a little. Nothing happened. "You think I'm doing it wrong?" he asked.

Luke shrugged. "You're the one who's done this before."

"Well, not really," Hayden admitted. "I mean, I saw it on TV once."

"Tell me you're kidding."

"What? It looked easy."

"Oh, God."

Hayden sighed. "Fine. New plan." He stuffed the card back into his pocket. "Put your shoulder into it."

"What?"

"The door. Come on. Give it a try."

"Bust the door open with my shoulder? You see that on TV, too?" But at Hayden's pleading look, Luke caved. "Fine." He took a couple steps back from the door. "I don't know why I'm doing this. You're bigger anyway," he muttered, then charged. He slammed his shoulder into the door. It hurt. A lot. And it was the same shoulder he'd slammed into the wall a few minutes ago. *Bad plan,* he thought as he bounced off the door. *Really bad plan.*

"Are you okay?" Hayden asked, eyes wide.

Luke sank down into a sitting position with his back against the door. He tested out his arm gingerly. "Ouch," he said finally.

Hayden started to laugh. Luke looked up at him incredulously, which only made Hayden laugh harder. "I'm sorry," he gasped. "I'm sorry. That just looked . . . really funny."

Luke started to laugh, too, less because it was funny than because it was so strange that Hayden found it so. "Yeah, well," he said after Hayden sat down next to him. "So much for your telescope."

"It's okay," Hayden said. "It was worth it just to see that. Like a fucking rubber ball."

Luke turned toward him. "Okay. Your turn," he said, which set them both off again.

Now, three years later, Luke climbed the stairs and stood in front of the locked white door. He wondered if he should charge it again. Maybe a few more years' worth of muscle would get the job done. But what good would it do to get it open now? Hayden wasn't there, and Luke didn't want to see the telescope without him. *We should have just taken astronomy,* he thought.

Luke sat down with his back against the door, just as before. He leaned his head back and closed his eyes, trying to imagine Hayden sitting next to him, trying to imagine being fourteen again. He'd thought that was the worst year of his life. Now he wasn't so sure.

CHAPTER 39

WHEN LUKE FINALLY headed back to his room on Monday night, it was dark out. The moon had sunk behind a cloud, and the tall lamp that usually illuminated the pathway to Luke's dormitory had been knocked out the day before by a low-flying football. He could barely see a foot in front of him.

All of a sudden, he felt himself collide with someone. He heard a yelp of surprise as the other person fell to the ground. "Sorry!" he said quickly, reaching out a hand to help the person up.

"Prescott?" came the voice from the ground, groping for Luke's hand. "Is that you?"

Luke knew that voice. "Albright." He tugged Cooper to his feet. Cooper looked even tinier than usual. Dark bags hung underneath his eyes. His body was stooped, and his shoulders were hunched. He looked terrible. "What are *you* up to?" Luke asked, staring him down.

"Going for a walk," Cooper said nonchalantly, starting to head past Luke.

Luke reached out and grabbed Cooper's arm, halting him. "Do that often in the middle of the night?" he asked darkly.

Cooper wrenched away. "What's that supposed to mean?"

"I bet you see some interesting stuff on those walks of yours," Luke pressed sarcastically. *Why am I being such a jerk?*

"So what if I do?" Cooper said defensively. "My prerogative. I mind my own business."

"How noble." Luke smirked. *Just leave the guy alone. This isn't about him.*

"You got something to say, then say it," Cooper challenged.

"Go fuck yourself," Luke said, temporarily unable to think up anything better to say.

"Touchy, touchy," Cooper clucked. "Somebody's time of the month?" Luke jerked forward, and Cooper sprang back. "Psycho."

"You want to know why you're out here all by yourself?" Luke asked. "I'll tell you. It's because nobody wants to be around you. Nobody gives a shit about you." Cooper took a halfhearted step toward him that looked more like a stumble than a challenge, and Luke laughed meanly. "What're you going to do? Keep your mouth shut at me? You're already doing that."

"You make your choices. I make mine."

"And if yours are spineless?" Luke spat back.

"That's for me to decide." Cooper's breath was heavy and thick. "And maybe I don't have a clue what the hell you're talking about," he tossed in as an afterthought.

"That's a load of crap, and you know it."

"Yeah? Where's your proof?"

"Where the fuck is your conscience?" Both boys' voices were raised now, and they paused for a second to make sure no one was about to come out, yell at them, and stop them from what they had to finish.

"You are disgusting, Albright," Luke whispered. "You really are, you know that? If you saw something, you have a . . . *responsibility* to come forward and say something."

"Oh yeah? And how's that 'coming forward' thing working for you?" Luke was silent. "Well, come on, tell me. Is life so great because you're doing the right thing? You getting the rewards you deserve?"

He's got a point.

Shut up.

"You should come forward," Luke quavered. His anger was turning to frustration, and he didn't feel quite as sure of himself as he had moments earlier.

"Didn't see anything." Cooper's voice was stubborn and certain. "Nothing to come forward about." Cooper started to walk away, his footsteps slow and weighted against the ground.

"I know you were there," Luke said, his voice as limp and tired as his body. He rubbed his hand roughly over the back of his neck.

"You don't know a thing," Cooper called back.

"I know you were there," Luke called after him, but Cooper was already gone.

CHAPTER 40

LUKE NEARLY DIDN'T RECOGNIZE his brother when he arrived for dinner on Tuesday. Growing up, although Jason was only a year older than Luke, he had always seemed infinitely bigger, infinitely stronger, infinitely better. But the Jason who showed up at the Grill was nothing like Luke remembered. His hair had grown out some, and it stuck out in tufts. He was wearing a red button-down flannel shirt over a white T-shirt, neither of which looked like they had been recently washed. It took Luke a second to register that this was, in fact, his brother. The last time Luke had seen Jason, he'd seemed at least somewhat together. Now he just looked like he'd lost his mind. It was actually a little embarrassing. Luke lifted up his hand in a jerky, awkward wave.

Jason reached his brother, and a hug, equally as awkward as the wave, was procured. "It's good to see you," he said, flashing Luke a lopsided grin. Jason looked like he hadn't shaved in weeks. Short brown hairs jutted out from his face as ugly reminders of how much had changed.

"Yeah, you too," Luke said, wondering if this new Jason would still be able to help him.

Luke and Jason headed into the Grill. "So how are you?" Jason asked, sitting down at a table in the back.

Luke took a seat. "I'm okay, I guess. How are things with you?"

"They're . . . I don't know. I guess I'm still figuring things out."

Luke nodded, nervous, stalling. "You ever talk to Mom about Stanford?"

Jason barked out a short laugh. "Yeah. That was interesting."

"I'll bet," Luke said dryly.

Jason shrugged. "No, but it's okay. She's letting me stay at home, and she's offered to get me a job at the bank. Whatever, maybe I'll take it. I'm still deciding."

"So you're definitely not going back to school?" Luke asked.

"Probably not."

Luke raised an eyebrow. "Wow. That's intense."

"Yeah." Jason scratched his head. "Well, you know. Things change."

The waiter came up to the table. Luke and Jason ordered burgers and fries, the only meal at the Grill that was halfway tolerable, and made small talk until the food arrived.

"So Hayden's trial starts tomorrow, huh?" Jason asked, finally breaking the unspoken barrier.

"Yeah. Murder in the first degree."

"Jesus."

"I didn't meet with his lawyer again," Luke said. "Didn't want him to pressure me." He looked up at his brother, almost guiltily.

"So you decided not to back him up?" Jason's face was unreadable.

"I haven't decided anything yet."

"Not a lot of time left, Luke," Jason said.

"Don't you think I know that?" Luke snapped. Jason raised an eyebrow and filled his mouth with hamburger. Luke took a long drink of water and swished it around in his mouth. He swallowed. "Sorry," he said.

"That's okay," Jason said, when it wasn't.

"Everything's just been kind of nuts."

"I get that," Jason said. "I do. I mean, I remember Hayden. I just can't believe . . ." Jason's voice trailed off.

"Yeah." Luke twirled a fry around in a glob of ketchup. "So what do you think?"

"What do I think . . . ?"

"About what I should do."

Jason spread out his palms. "Well, I mean, I can't really . . ."

Yes, you can.

His brother sighed. "I guess I think . . . well . . . you can't lose sight of the fact that a guy is dead. So don't do this because you feel like you owe Hayden something. If you back him up, do it because you think it's the right thing. But you don't owe him anything."

"What the fuck kind of answer is that?"

Jason looked a little surprised. "Since when do you swear?"

Luke shrugged. "You're avoiding the question." He paused. "What if it were one of your friends?"

"It isn't," Jason said stiffly.

"Well, what if it were?" Luke insisted. "What would you do in my place?"

"I don't know, Luke. I'm not in your place."

Luke kicked his foot into the leg of the table. His glass of water sloshed over. "What help are you?" He looked away, trying to calm himself. He grabbed a napkin and started to mop up the water. "I'm sorry," he said, turning back to his brother. He set down the napkin.

"You seem to be saying that a lot tonight," Jason said quietly.

"I know, I just . . ." Luke rubbed his hand across the back of his neck.

"Dad used to do that." Jason nodded toward Luke's hand. "When he was mad about something."

Luke pulled his hand away like it was on fire. "I don't want to talk about Dad."

"We never talk about Dad."

"So?" Luke popped a fry into his mouth.

"So we have to talk about it sometime."

"Why? Not talking about it has been working pretty well for the past couple of years."

"You know it hasn't. We can't keep dodging it. I mean, he's gone and—"

"His choice."

"It wasn't like that," Jason said. "You know it was way more complicated than that."

"Bullshit. It wasn't that complicated."

"He was having a really hard time, Luke," Jason attempted.

"Everyone's life is hard, but not everyone . . ." Luke trailed off. "I don't want to talk about this."

"He lost control of things."

Luke said nothing.

"He loved us, Luke."

"Funny way of showing it." Luke felt like he was about to cry, and he was embarrassed, and he was beginning to despise Jason for making him feel this way. *This wasn't what I wanted you to come here to talk about.*

"He was sick, Luke. He was depressed."

"Shut up, Jason." Luke's voice was barely audible.

"He was taking medication. But he went off it for a couple of weeks."

"Shut up, Jason," Luke growled.

"He thought he was getting better, but going off the meds made him do it."

"SHUT UP, JASON! JUST SHUT THE FUCK UP!" Luke lunged across the table at his brother, knocking over both glasses of water and sending his own plate crashing to the floor. Jason jumped back, overturning his chair with a crash. Luke fell forward onto the table, missing Jason.

"Hey! Hey!" The waiter came running over, pulling Luke back. "What the hell is the matter with you?"

"Sorry! I'm sorry!" Luke stepped back, away from his brother.

"It was my fault," Jason told the waiter. "It really was." He pulled out his wallet and tossed a clump of bills on the table. "We're sorry. We're leaving," he stammered, and they rushed out the door.

Outside the restaurant, Luke and Jason stood for a moment without speaking. "I didn't mean to . . ." Luke's voice faded away.

Jason scuffed his shoes against the ground. "I know. I'm sorry I said that stuff. I just wanted you . . . to understand, you know?"

"Jason—"

"No, forget it. I just thought—well, it doesn't matter now." Jason swallowed hard.

They waited outside for a second. "I should get going," Luke said finally.

"I'm sorry I wasn't more help."

Luke shrugged. "Not your job."

Jason's face twisted, like he was trying to decide whether or not to say something. "Listen, Mom told me about what happened when she came to see you."

Luke's face burned. "What I said . . ."

"You were a dick for saying that stuff."

Luke tried not to care. "Yeah, well."

"She told *me* about it. That's how upset she was," Jason pressed.

"Hey, how is this helpful? I'm a little stressed out right now, in case you haven't noticed. So if you're not going to help me, then you might as well leave me alone." He glared at his older brother.

"Fine," said Jason. "Fine." He exhaled loudly. "But what she did, it wasn't her fault, not really. So at some point you're going to have to forgive her. And when you do, you better hope she forgives you, too."

CHAPTER 41

IT WAS LATE when Luke got back to the dorm. The room was a mess, but he was too angry to care. Too angry and too scared. He squeezed his eyes shut. *This is ridiculous. This is not useful.* Luke snatched up the bag by the door that contained his things for the shower and left the room. He strode purposefully down the hall. The thought of finally doing something productive kept his feet moving.

Right. Left. Right. Left.

Why am I the one who has to deal with all of this? I didn't do anything wrong.

Right. Left. Right. Left.

Did I do anything wrong?

Right. Left. Right. Left.

Hayden endangered everyone up on that cliff. He was rash and careless and stupid. How could he do this? How could he be so thoughtless?

Right. Left. Right. Left.

Or was he? Had it all been planned out? Did he mean to kill Russell on that cliff?

Right. Left. Right. Left.

When I walked in on him before, when he was lying in the room, look-
ing all pensive and creepy, was he planning it then? Was that the moment,
and I just missed it? Was he deciding how he was going to kill Russell and
make it look like an accident? Is that who Hayden is?

Luke reached the showers. The bathroom, thank God, was
empty. He didn't think he could deal with another person right
now. He stepped inside a shower and stripped off his clothes, dumping them in a heap outside the shower stall. He turned on the water, letting it run over him.

He reeled back and smacked his open palm against the wall.
Pain shot through his wrist, and a crack resounded through the
empty shower room. The sound reverberated off the walls, flying
back at him like a boomerang. Yet Luke found the sound relaxing,
and he repeated the action, this time hitting the wall with a closed
fist. The sound was not as loud, not as satisfying. His hand began to
throb. Ignoring it, he tried again, hitting harder. Still not as good.
Again. Again.

His right fist smashed against the smooth white tile, and his
hand scraped mercilessly against the rough grout between the tiles.
Lightning slashed up from his knuckles to his arm, synapse after
synapse. The pain was dizzying, and he leaned against the wall to
catch his breath. Each drop of water burrowed into his hand, feeling
like hot needles. He reached up with his left hand and turned off the
shower spout. The last few drops sprayed down on him, and Luke
fought the urge to flinch as they taunted his shoulders and back.

He looked down at the floor of the shower. The water dripping
off his body was lined with blood now, tainted crimson from his fist.

It pooled by the drain and slid in, a river of red that was slowly disappearing. Luke brought his fist up into his line of vision. The side of his hand was starting to swell, the skin raw and bleeding. The smooth skin on top of his knuckles was shredded. He touched it gingerly with his left palm, his hand coming away bloody. It hurt like hell. *Stupid.*

Luke stepped out of the shower. He grabbed a towel, wrapped it around his hand, and pressed until the blood stopped flowing. He removed the towel and stared at it. The white cloth was caked with red streaks that wrapped around in a circle where he'd held it to his mangled hand.

Sometimes Luke wondered where his father had gotten the handgun. They'd never kept guns in the house. Had he bought it on the street somewhere? He wondered if his father had had to learn how to use it, if he had ever fired it before he brought it to his temple.

Sometimes Luke wondered about his father's coworker, the woman who'd found him. He wondered what that had been like. There must have been so much blood. It must have literally coated the floor. The woman must have stepped in it. It must have stained her shoes. She must have screamed.

Sometimes Luke wondered if his father had screamed. Had it been too quick for even that? Had his father died right away, or had there been a couple seconds, after the gunshot, when he could feel the pain? If that were so, had he regretted it? Had he regretted what he'd done to his wife, to his sons? Had he understood what it would do to them? Did he even care?

CHAPTER 42

LUKE AWOKE ALONE in his room on Wednesday morning, overwhelmingly tempted to just stay there in that bed, to pretend his alarm hadn't gone off. Not face it, ever. He might have done just that if it hadn't been for a knock at the door.

Reluctantly, he forced his leaden legs to lift him off his bed. He pulled the door open a crack and blinked into the lit hallway, momentarily blinded. "Morning," the blurry figure in front of him said, stepping through the doorway and flipping a switch to fill the room with light.

"Hey, Rachel." Even blurry, she was pretty. Luke pulled his throbbing hand behind his back so that she wouldn't see it.

"So I wanted to know if you needed a ride to the courthouse."

Luke blinked. "But your car . . ." . . . *got smashed into a tree . . .*

"My parents got me another one," she said with a shrug. "Few days ago."

"Oh," he said. His eyes were beginning to adjust, and Rachel was coming beautifully into focus. "Cool."

"I hate it," she replied dully. "I miss the old one."

"Oh."

"So Tristan and I, we're leaving in like half an hour."

"You're going?"

She reddened. "Well, Tristan's going to be a character witness, and I thought, you know, I'd be there for him."

"Right."

"Yeah. And you, I mean, if you want." She looked away. "Do you want to come with us?"

"Yeah, okay." He'd been planning to take the bus, but this would be easier. Plus, Rachel. Luke looked down at his pajamas. "I have to get dressed."

"Meet us in the lot?" Rachel asked, sounding a little too relieved.

"All right."

It was eight o'clock when Luke met Tristan and Rachel in the parking lot, and the sun was struggling out from beneath dark, heavy clouds. Rain was unavoidable. "Hey," Luke said in greeting, tucking his hand casually behind his hip again.

Too late. "What happened to your hand?" Rachel asked, taking a step toward Luke. "It looks bad."

Luke inched a little bit farther away. "Hit it on something."

"Something like a buzz saw?" Tristan asked. "Man!"

"You should get that checked out. By, like, a doctor or someone. It could be broken," said Rachel.

"Can you just drop it?" Luke muttered, more unkindly than he'd meant to.

"Okay." Rachel looked hurt. Luke turned away, embarrassed, and climbed into Rachel's new BMW.

Tristan sat in back, periodically fiddling with his tie, his newly healed leg stretched out across the back seat. Rachel's eyes were glued to the road. The silence was earsplitting. "So," Tristan said finally, "Luke?"

"Yeah?"

"I was just wondering, you know, if you thought about what you were gonna say on the stand."

"Oh."

There was a pause. "Well," Tristan asked uncomfortably, "have you?"

Just leave me alone, Tristan. "Yeah, I have." *Of course I've thought about it. I can't seem to stop thinking about it.*

Another pause. "So . . . what are you going to say?"

Shut up, shut up, just be quiet. I don't want to talk about this. "I don't know yet."

Rachel took her eyes off the road for a minute to raise an eyebrow at Luke. "Look, Luke, I don't mean to be rude, but we're sort of on the way there. Don't you think you should know by now?"

Probably. Luke shrugged.

"It's not that hard a decision," Tristan said a little too loudly.

"You weren't there," Luke said stiffly.

"It doesn't matter!" Tristan exploded. "Hayden is your best friend! Or did that slip your mind?"

"Yeah, Tristan, it must have slipped my mind when I was carrying Russell's dead body out of Briar Lake! That's when it must have slipped my fucking mind!" Luke yelled back.

"Guys . . ." Rachel said nervously.

"Oh, so this is your solution? You think if Hayden goes to jail that Russell's gonna get resurrected?"

"No!" Luke said, frustrated. "I just—"

"You just what, Luke? 'Cause there's gotta be a pretty good reason you're willing to let your friend rot away in jail for the rest of his life."

"C'mon, Tris," Rachel said, swallowing hard, "let him be."

"Why the hell should I?" Tristan shouted. "Hayden is my friend, too!"

Luke laughed meanly. "Oh, is he? Is he really?"

"Yes!"

"You're pathetic. You're so fucking pathetic, you don't even know!"

"Hey!" Rachel broke in. "Look, all your fighting is distracting, and one car crash is enough for me, okay?"

The three fell silent, the memory of the accident all too vivid in their minds. But those were different times. Luke remembered the party, when he'd run into a drunken Russell on the second story. He'd asked him if he had a ride home. He'd wanted to make sure that Russell would be okay.

Suddenly Luke had a terribly evil thought. If Russell hadn't had a ride, if Russell had tried to drive himself and had killed himself, none of this would have ever been a problem. If Russell could have only died a few weeks earlier, Hayden wouldn't have had anything to do with it.

Finally, they arrived at the courthouse. There were some reporters out front, which Luke realized he should have expected, given who Hayden's father was. He tuned out the things the reporters shouted as he walked past them, but he did hear his name a few times. *They know who I am. They know what I'm here for. Everybody knows.*

Rachel went into the courtroom, but Luke and Tristan were herded into a large waiting room for witnesses. Because they were going to testify, they weren't allowed to hear the rest of the trial. They walked into the room together, but immediately split apart. Tristan headed over toward a couple of people from the fencing team who were still supporting Hayden and acting as character witnesses. Luke, unsure of what to do, went to stand near some vending machines in the corner.

There weren't many people in the room. Some of Luke's classmates were there, a couple of teachers, some men in police uniforms. *This is a big deal,* Luke thought stupidly. *This is a really big deal.*

He spotted Drew over in the corner talking to Nicole. Luke knew why Nicole was there, but he couldn't imagine why Drew would be. Luke was pretty sure that Drew wouldn't be one of Hayden's character witnesses.

He tried to pretend he hadn't seen them, to avoid the awkwardness that would have to follow, but Drew had nodded to him and was striding over. *What is he doing?*

"Hey," said Drew.

"Hey," Luke answered warily.

"So you're testifying. I assumed you would be." Drew's voice was not friendly, but it was not unfriendly either.

"Yeah."

"The district attorney wanted me to testify about what happened in the locker room. Back when Russell said that stuff about Hayden's dad."

"And Hayden started screaming that he'd kill him," Luke said, remembering.

"Yeah," said Drew. "That's—yeah."

Luke nodded.

"You know . . ." Drew shrugged uncomfortably. "I mean, I know what you think, but it's not like I don't like Hayden. I mean, he's still my friend." Luke said nothing. "But he killed somebody. So. Hey, I'm just telling the truth."

Then Luke recognized the look on Drew's face. It was guilt. "You don't have to explain it to me," said Luke. "You have your reasons." *Your reasons for being such an ass. For not standing by your friend.*

Like I did?

"I know I don't," Drew said staunchly. "I'm just saying."

"So don't," Luke answered.

"Fine. You want to be a tool? Fine."

"I'm a tool?" Luke said incredulously. "After the way you've been acting? I'm the tool?"

Drew held up his hands. "Hey, we came to check on you *the day after it happened.* We all tried. You told us to get lost."

"Oh, please," Luke scoffed. "You weren't there for me; you were there for all the gory details. You wanted the story."

Drew hesitated. "So what if we did? You don't think we had a right to know?"

Luke smacked his forehead with the palm of his hand. "You're right. With Russell having just died and Hayden being in jail, I should have been thinking about *you.* What was wrong with me?"

"Hey, say what you want, but we were there. You could have talked to us."

"Oh, yeah." Luke rolled his eyes. "Just join right in. You guys in your little pack. You strutting around like . . ." *Like Hayden.*

"He was gone," Drew hissed. "Why shouldn't . . . ? He was gone."

"Yeah," said Luke. "He's gone. I'm gone. You can have it."

"Have what?" Drew said flatly.

"I never wanted it," Luke told him.

Drew started to back away. "I don't know what you're talking about," he said. "You're weird, you know that?" He left.

Luke turned to the vending machine. He didn't really want chips or candy, the only options, but he needed something to do. He had no money in his pockets, though, so he started to feel a little silly. "Hey." He turned and Tristan was standing there. "What was . . . I mean, was that okay?" Tristan nodded back toward Drew. Luke shrugged. "Look, I'm sorry about what I said in the car. I mean, you don't have to . . . You can wait with us." He gestured back to where Luke's former teammates were standing.

"I'm fine." *I don't need you to feel sorry for me.*

Tristan groaned. "What is it with you, huh?"

"What?"

"I don't know. I know you're having a rough time. I'm trying to help. I get that I suck at it, but I'm trying."

"I never asked for your help," said Luke.

"You're my friend. You don't need to."

The niceness of it all was like being punched in the face. *I don't deserve this from you.* Luke gave a strangled laugh. "I'm not your friend. I was never your friend."

Tristan looked startled. "We're teammates. We're . . ."

"How many times did you and I eat lunch together before all of this? How many afternoons did we spend hanging out together on the quad? How many times did you and I stay up late talking about absolutely nothing?"

Tristan shifted awkwardly. "I mean, fine. Doesn't mean I don't want to help you, that I'm not, you know, there for you, or whatever. I mean, we hang out now all the time."

"I like your girlfriend," Luke said loudly, and it was like finally exhaling.

Tristan didn't miss a beat. "I trust her. I trust you."

You fucking doormat. "You shouldn't," Luke exclaimed in frustration, though it felt like kicking a puppy. "You shouldn't want to help me. You shouldn't give a crap about me, because I've been an ass to you."

"No, Luke, you—"

"You think we're *friends?* God, you are tragic." Luke stepped toward Tristan and got right in his face. "You know what your problem is?" he hissed. "You're weak."

Tristan stared at him. "You're in a bad place right now," he said, his voice level. "You're under a lot of pressure, a lot of stress. If you need me, you know where to find me."

Luke watched Tristan walk back to where his teammates were standing. He felt a twisting feeling in his stomach. *I'm not his friend. But I wish I were.*

CHAPTER 43

TRISTAN TESTIFIED late into the morning. Drew and Nicole and about half the people in the room had their turns in the afternoon. Eventually a bailiff came to tell them that court had been adjourned for the day and Hayden's trial would pick up again tomorrow. For Luke, it felt like a stay of execution: He hadn't been ready. The powers that be had known it.

On the way back from the courthouse, Luke leaned his head against the side of the car, his head smacking against the window with every jolt of the road. He knew he should lift up his head. A dull ache was pooling under the skin, waiting to break out in a storm of pain that would turn Luke's brain into scrambled eggs. All he would have to do to stop it from surfacing would be to move his head, sit up straight, and lean his head back against the soft cushioning of the seat. Luke didn't move.

His father had gotten those, the headaches. Migraines. Luke hadn't really understood them when he was younger. Everything would be normal, and suddenly his dad would disappear into his study. When that happened, Luke and Jason weren't allowed to knock on the study door or make any loud noises. When they were little, their mother used to send them outside with a football or a bat and baseball and tell them to come inside in an hour or so. "When Daddy's feeling better," she'd say. "Daddy isn't feeling well again. Go outside and play."

Banished from their home without truly understanding why, the brothers abandoned the restrictions of baseball and football and invented their own games with the tools nature had provided them. Their toys were the flat stones and fallen nuts of the yard, anything that the gardeners had missed in their weekly visits. When they were finally called inside, usually around dinnertime, their father would be waiting with a big smile on his face. And looking at him then, Luke and Jason would almost be able to pretend that there was nothing wrong at all with their father.

Luke tore his head away from the side of the car. "Pull over," he said through clenched teeth.

Rachel looked over from the driver's seat. "What?"

"Pull over," Luke said, already starting to open the door.

Confused, Rachel pulled the car over to the side of the road, and Luke shoved the car door the rest of the way open and leaned forward, his seat belt still pulling him into the seat.

"What's going on?" Tristan asked, sticking his head between the front seats. "Luke, you okay?"

Luke answered by throwing up into the dirt on the side of the road. When he was finished, he hung there by the seat belt. He felt a tentative hand on his back that was quickly withdrawn.

Tristan's voice. "Um, Luke?"

Rachel's voice. "Are you all right?"

Luke closed his eyes for a moment, trying to let everything he was feeling drip out over his arched back down to the ground and leave him forever. When it didn't, just as he had expected, Luke shot his eyes open and sat upright. "Fine. I'm fine. Let's go." He nodded to Rachel.

She hesitated. "Luke . . ."

Luke slammed the door shut. "Let's go."

Rachel pulled the car back onto the road. "Do you, uh, need a doctor or something?"

"Let's just go home," Luke said simply.

"Yeah, okay." Rachel was unnerved.

"You should rest," Tristan offered from the back seat. "Get some sleep, and maybe you'll feel better."

"Yeah." Luke couldn't handle Tristan acting so friendly, like nothing had ever happened. It just made him feel worse. He had already wished about a thousand times that he hadn't said all those mean things to Tristan. *He just wanted to be my friend. Why couldn't I let him?*

The rhythm of the road took over for a time. Luke's nausea began to subside. Exhaustion took over. His eyes were drifting shut just as they passed by the Forest County Post Office, where most Briar students had their mail sent. "Hey," said Tristan. "Hey, pull over."

The car slowed. "What?" Rachel asked.

"Can we stop for a sec?"

"Why?"

"My letter. From the University of Chicago. It might be there."

"Check online," said Rachel.

"No way! I don't want to find out like that."

"Oh my God, if you got in, it'll be good either way, and if you didn't, it'll suck either way."

"I'll be really quick," Tristan promised.

"This is so not a good time," protested Rachel. "Luke's sick. He needs to get home. What's the matter with you?"

"Aw, come on. It'll take me like five minutes. Luke doesn't mind, right, Luke?"

Actually, Luke did mind. He minded very much. He was tired and stressed, and he'd just puked on the side of the highway. But he knew what a big deal the letter was to Tristan, and right now if Tristan had asked him for his firstborn child, he would have given it to him.

It was also possible that one of Luke's own letters might have come, and he was just a little bit curious as to where he'd be spending the next four years of his life. He hadn't checked online yet; the Internet had not been kind to him the first time. "No," he said. "I don't mind."

Tristan laughed and clapped him on the shoulder. "Thanks, man." Luke felt even guiltier.

Rachel turned and gave Luke a quizzical stare. He just shrugged. She sighed and turned the car into the post office parking lot. "Five minutes."

"You don't even have to come in," Tristan pointed out as he and Luke stepped out of the car.

"Wasn't planning on it," she snapped back.

"Fine," said Tristan. He started off toward the post office with Luke trailing after him. "Appreciate the support, by the way!" he called to her over his shoulder.

Unfortunately, Tristan's letter had not arrived and, dismayed, he headed for the door. Luke checked his own mail, and though there was nothing from colleges, he did have one letter. "Read it on the way back to the car," Tristan advised, "or Rachel will kill us."

As they walked through the parking lot, Luke examined the return address. It was from Hayden's lawyer, Martin Barnes. Luke opened the envelope and anger surged through him. "Son of a bitch."

Tristan spun around. "What?"

Luke pulled a photograph out of the envelope. "It's from the lawyer."

Tristan picked up the photograph and stared at it. After a second, he nodded. "Okay. That's cheap."

The photograph had been taken a few months earlier, at Briar Academy's annual Halloween dance. In the picture were Hayden, Luke, and Nicole. (Not pictured was the date Hayden had set Luke up with, a slightly trashy junior who had been kicked out of the dance and suspended for getting wasted and propositioning the wood shop teacher.) In the photo Hayden, dressed as Zorro, had one arm around Luke's shoulders and the other around Nicole's waist. Luke and Hayden were looking at each other and laughing. "Yeah. Cheap."

There was no card. Just the photo.

"Hey, Rachel?" Luke said, leaning in to the side of the car. "Can we make one more stop before we head home?"

She threw up her hands in disgust. "What am I, a freaking taxi?"

"It's really important," said Luke.

"Where do you want to go?" she asked.

"To visit Hayden."

"Luke, that's like a million miles out of our way!"

"Please, if you'll just drop me off, I'll take the bus home. It's really, really important."

Rachel stared at him for a moment. She must have seen some trace of desperation on his face, because she sighed and flashed him a wry smile. "All right. Get in. Your friendly neighborhood taxi is ready to go."

"Oh, sure, *now* it's fine," said Tristan, not quite joking.

"Shut up, Tristan," said Rachel.

CHAPTER 44

"LUKE, IT'S GOOD to see you," said Hayden as he entered the blue room. "How—"

"What the fuck is this?" Luke interrupted, standing up. He slammed the photograph down on the table. "You think you can guilt-trip me, remind of some stupid dance, and that'll make it all okay?" *How dare he. How* dare *he.*

"What are you talking about?" Hayden asked, picking up the photograph.

"Don't try to be, like, coy, or whatever," said Luke. "I know you had your lawyer send this to me."

"What? No. I didn't. I don't know anything about this."

Luke laughed coldly. "Yeah, right. I'm not falling for that crap. This is a cheap trick, and you know it."

"I had nothing to do with it!" Hayden protested. "My lawyer must have done it. He's a good guy, Luke, but he can be kind of a sleaze. Look, I'm serious. I didn't even know about it. I wouldn't try to pressure you like that." His eyes bored into Luke, begging him to understand. "I swear."

Luke rolled his eyes. "You swear. You swear, you swear, you swear."

Hayden blinked, confused.

"I don't know if I believe you," Luke said, suddenly matter-of-factly.

Hayden set his jaw. "I see."

Luke sat down, and after a moment Hayden did the same. "I just don't know if I trust you," Luke said, and both boys knew he wasn't talking about the photograph anymore.

"But you used to," Hayden pointed out.

"Yeah."

"You used to trust me."

"Yeah."

"Do you remember when you stopped?" Hayden's voice caught on the last word, and he looked away.

"When Russell died," said Luke. *I'm lying. It was before that.* "Actually, it was before that."

"Oh. I see." Hayden cleared his throat and spoke slowly, drawing each word out, syllable by syllable. "So you think I murdered him. You think—just like the rest of them—that I went up there planning to kill him and I pushed him off and now I'm so fucking happy about it. That's what you think."

"Why did you push him, Hayden?"

"To kill him, of course," Hayden snapped. "To kill him and then head off to twirl my mustache and tie pretty girls to railroad tracks."

"Hayden."

"What? I know it's what you all think. So here it is—my

fucking confession! I killed him on purpose! That's what you want to hear, right, Luke? So consider this my early Christmas present to you."

"Hayden—"

"Let me guess, you don't believe me. Well, what do you want from me, Luke? I tell you I didn't do it, you say you don't believe me. I tell you I did do it, and you don't believe me either. What do you want me to tell you?"

"The truth!" Luke exploded. "I want you to tell me the truth!"

"The truth?" Hayden laughed, and the laugh was rich and controlled. "Since when does the truth make any difference? No one wants to hear the truth. Everyone just wants a good story. Jealous ex-boyfriend murders girl's new lover—now, that's a good story."

"Cut the crap, Hayden."

"No, I would watch that on pay-per-view, wouldn't you?"

"Stop it," said Luke.

"I can't!" screamed Hayden suddenly, and Luke jumped in his seat. "I can't stop it! It doesn't go away! He's dead, and he's dead, and it doesn't go away!" Hayden stood and shoved his chair back into the table. Metal hit metal with a clang. "I pushed him! And he's dead, and they're going to crucify me for it! I can't stop it!"

The guard rushed into the room. "Is everything all right in here?" he asked.

Hayden fell silent and stared down at the floor. "Yeah, everything's fine," said Luke. The guard fixed him with a stern look. Luke gulped. "But I should . . . I guess I should go." He stood and walked toward the door, then turned back to Hayden, who was hunched over, staring at his feet. "Hayden, was it an accident?" Luke asked.

Hayden looked up. "Of course.'

"Goodbye," said Luke.

"Goodbye," said Hayden.

CHAPTER 45

HEADMASTER GRUNBERG came to his door that evening. "Luke. Glad I caught you."

"Come on in." Luke backed away and pulled out the desk chair for the headmaster to sit.

The headmaster entered but shook his head at the chair. "No, no, I won't keep you long. I just wanted to, well, make sure you were all right. With everything. I mean for tomorrow." He squinted up at Luke. "I know you didn't get a chance to testify today. And everything being drawn out . . . it could make things harder."

"I'm fine," Luke lied. He didn't feel like talking right now. He felt like getting out of the building. It was suffocating him.

"It's difficult, I know," said the old man.

You don't know. You don't have a fucking clue. "Yeah."

"Well, if you want to talk—"

"I don't," Luke interrupted. He blushed. "I'm not trying to be rude."

The old man nodded. "I understand. It's all right."

"It's not all right," Luke mumbled. "I shouldn't have . . . I mean, I appreciate you coming here. I've just got a lot I'm dealing with, and . . ."

"Yes. Well." The old man coughed into his hand. "I shouldn't have bothered you." He paused and laughed sadly. "Maybe *I* just needed someone to talk to." He started to leave.

"Wait," Luke said, curious. "Why do you need someone to talk to?"

The headmaster turned and shrugged. "Everyone's blaming Hayden over what happened when really . . . Well, it's really more my fault than anyone's."

Luke was stunned. "How's it your fault?"

The old man smiled wanly. "I knew what you boys were doing. The jumping, I mean. Half the faculty did." He sighed. "The Conrads are suing the school, you know."

"I didn't know that."

"Yes." The old man rubbed his eyes with a gnarled hand and took a deep breath. "I never thought anyone would get hurt. I could have put a stop to it, and I didn't. I was stupid, and a child died on my watch." He stared at Luke, thinking. "You boys, it's not so much your fault as mine."

"Do you think Hayden should be let off?" Luke asked.

"I don't know. I don't know what happened up there."

"Neither do I," Luke said.

"Is that how you're going to testify?" he asked.

"I'm not sure what I'm going to say yet."

"When the time comes, you'll know," said Headmaster Grunberg.

"What if I don't?" Luke asked.

The old man chuckled grimly. "Then I'm wrong again. But I

think you'll know when the time comes. Sometimes it just works like that." He tried to give Luke a reassuring look. "Good luck," he said, and was gone.

Luke had to get out of the room.

He knew from the minute that he left the dorm that he was heading for the cliff, but along the way he distracted himself by thinking about his brother. It had been so jarring the last time he had seen him. He'd looked so . . . not together. *But he'll figure it out,* Luke told himself. *Jason always does.*

He felt a sudden surge of anger then, thinking of his brother sitting at home in Springfield on a couch in one of the various sitting rooms. It was more than anger, though, Luke realized. It was jealousy. Luke wished he could sit back like his brother and watch the world go by. He wished he could go somewhere where no one could find him and no one could ask him any questions. He wished he didn't have to go to court the next day.

Luke wondered what would happen if he just didn't go. What would happen if they called his name and he just wasn't there? Would they try to find him? Would they drag him to the courthouse? Would they arrest him?

And all of a sudden the cliff was in front of him. He stared up at it, eyeing it like a rival. Part of Luke wanted to turn and run, but he forced himself to climb. He needed to do this. He didn't know why, but he needed to do this.

Someone had painted a large cross on top of the rocks. It stretched over almost the entire area. Luke wondered who had put it there, then decided it didn't matter. He wondered if Russell had been religious.

Luke didn't want to stand on top of the cross, so he moved

slowly around it, his eyes glued to his sneakers. Finally he was standing at the edge, staring directly down at the rocks below. They pointed up at him like blackened teeth. A tongue of lake water swirled through them as if preparing for a meal. Luke swallowed hard, and he began to remember.

He remembered finding Russell's body by the rocks. He remembered the way that Russell's blond hair had matted darkly around his head like a net, with a few sticky tendrils drifting outward. He remembered how when he'd touched Russell, his hand had come away bloody, and he'd seen how the blood was just rushing out of Russell's head, twisting like worms into the water until finally disappearing in the darkness.

Luke's stomach lurched, but he didn't close his eyes. He forced himself to keep looking down at the rocks. He knew that they must have been the last thing Russell saw before the end. He wondered if Russell realized he was going to die and tried to catch himself on anything, or if he just closed his eyes and let it happen, thinking maybe he'd be all right.

Luke stood on the cliff for a long time, watching the night play over and over again in his mind. Russell arguing with Hayden. Hayden pushing Russell. Russell falling. Could he have prevented it? Maybe he could have tried harder to stop the argument. Maybe he could have grabbed Russell before he fell.

Maybe he could have been somewhere else that night. Maybe he could have made sure Hayden and Russell were, too.

CHAPTER 46

WALKING BACK DOWN, Luke was so caught up in his own head that he almost didn't see Cooper Albright sitting with his back against a tree at the bottom of the cliff. He looked as if he were drowning in his oversize sweatshirt and jeans. Staring down at him, Luke realized how small Cooper really was. Cooper's head jerked up suddenly as Luke approached. "Jesus," he said, "you startled me."

Luke stopped a few feet away. He glanced back up at the cliff. There was a clear view to the top. "You must have seen me up there," he pointed out.

Cooper coughed and stood. "Yeah. Yeah. I was just gonna leave before you . . . I guess I lost track of . . ." He laughed curtly. "Yeah." Cooper's voice was different. It was lower and fuller. Less creepy, more tired.

"Are you following me?" Luke asked, unsettled.

"No!" Cooper's green eyes widened in surprise. "No, I didn't even know you were gonna be out here. I'm not, like, stalking you."

"Come out here to get stoned?" Luke asked.

"I'm not stoned."

"What are you doing here, then?" he asked, almost friendly.

"None of your fucking business."

"Fine." Luke started to walk away. He had too much to think about tonight without wasting his time talking to Cooper.

"You ever dream about it?" Cooper called after him. Luke turned around. "Because I dream about it all the time. Like every night." Cooper was staring down at the dirt. "You ever dream about it?"

"Yeah," Luke said hoarsely.

"You were right," said Cooper. "I lied. I did see it."

Every muscle in Luke's body tensed simultaneously. "What did you see?"

"I was right here," Cooper whispered. He kicked the dirt. "I was standing right here. Came out to smoke some weed. I hid when I heard you guys coming because I wasn't sure who you were and I thought, you know, maybe you were someone coming to bust me or something. And then, once you were up there, I came out again, and I heard you guys arguing, and I looked up just as it happened . . . And the sound was so loud. When he hit. It was so loud." A tear rolled down Cooper's cheek. "Just a few yards away. I saw when he . . . the rocks . . ." Angrily, Cooper brushed off his face. "I ran."

Luke didn't know what to say. What was Cooper expecting with this little confession? What did he want from Luke? "It's okay," Luke offered, though of course it wasn't. "You got scared."

"I didn't know what to do," Cooper said, his voice thick and low. "I didn't want people to ask me about it. I didn't want to have to talk about it."

Neither did I.

"It was so easy. Like, you have no idea how easy. Nobody ever knew I was even there." He shrugged. "I just figured, I mean, you saw it, and that'd be enough for the police, so why did I have to say anything? If I said I was there, I'd have to tell them about what I saw and I just couldn't do that."

"I had to," Luke said, glaring at Cooper. "I had to do that. I had to tell them everything." His voice was so quiet he could barely hear himself speak. "Why should you get to keep quiet and not me? Why should I have to talk to the police and testify in court while you sit around smoking pot?"

"I don't know."

Luke inhaled deeply, partly because he needed time to collect his thoughts and partly because it was the only thing keeping him from hitting Cooper in the stomach. "Do you have any idea what I've been through? What I'm going to have to do tomorrow? They're going to ask me to incriminate my best friend."

Cooper stiffened. "I've been through hell, too, you know. Not being able to talk to anyone about this. Do you have any idea what that's like?"

"You could still go to the cops," Luke pressed. "You could tell them what you saw."

"What would be the point? They already talked to you. Shit, the trial started already. It's too late."

You could answer the question instead of me. You could tell them so I don't have to. You could choose so I don't have to. "It's the right thing to do," Luke said simply.

Cooper turned away from Luke, back toward the cliff. He

didn't say anything for a long time, and Luke began to think the conversation was over. Then, "He screamed. Do you remember? Before the rocks. He just screamed, and it was so loud until he hit."

"Cooper, tell me about before," Luke said abruptly.

Cooper turned back toward Luke. "What?"

"Tell me about before he fell. When he was up on the cliff with me and Hayden. Tell me about when Hayden pushed him."

Cooper looked at him with confusion. "You were up there. You saw it happen."

"Tell me anyway." Luke was starting to feel frantic. "Tell me about when Hayden pushed him. Was it why he fell? Was it Hayden's fault?"

"I was too far away," Cooper said. "Too far to see."

"You knew Hayden only used one hand when he pushed Russell. How would you have known that if you didn't see? You did see—don't lie to me. Tell me the truth."

Cooper squeezed his eyes shut and then opened them again. "The truth is, I don't know. I don't know if Hayden killed him. I saw him push Russell, I saw Russell fall, but I don't know if it was an accident. I don't know it any better than you do. I'm sorry."

Luke sat down on the ground, crushed. "What do I tell them?" he asked Cooper. "Do I say that Hayden was responsible? Or do I say that he wasn't and just let him off the hook?"

"I don't know."

Luke snorted. "I didn't even like Russell."

"Not a lot of people did."

"Yeah."

"I think he liked it that way." Cooper tugged on the collar of his sweatshirt. "Being hated. I think he liked it. It meant that people noticed him, knew who he was. He liked pissing people off."

"He was obnoxious," Luke pointed out.

"He was an *asshole*."

"I still can't believe he's gone."

"Me either."

Luke was suddenly aware of how dark it was. The night had snuck up on them. The blackness tore savagely into the conversation, and Luke felt suddenly afraid. Going back to the cliff was one thing, but going back at night? It was creepy. "I should get back," he said.

Cooper nodded. "Yeah. Okay."

"You coming?"

"Later," he said. "I'm not done yet."

"Done doing what?" Luke asked.

"Remembering," said Cooper.

"Oh." Luke understood. "All right. Then I'll see you later." He began to head off, then turned back. "Uh, you know," Luke started, his face reddening. "If you want to, like, talk about stuff, about Russell, I'm around. You know, whenever."

"Yeah. Me too. I mean, if you need to talk about it."

"Yeah."

As Luke approached the dormitory, the fear that had grabbed him in the woods began to subside. This was not the time for fear. He had not earned the right to cower yet. There was still too much he had to do, too much he had to think about. He couldn't be Cooper. He couldn't hide. He couldn't be Jason either. He couldn't sit back, apart from the world, afraid to dive into it.

Luke was different from them, he realized, and it made him feel stronger. He could do what was asked of him. He could make decisions and he could live his life and he could face his fears. He could handle difficulty. He could handle pain. He could wake up tomorrow, go to court, and say whatever it was he decided to say. That was what set him apart from Cooper, from Jason—and from his father.

CHAPTER 47

LUKE MET RACHEL in the parking lot the next morning and was surprised to see she was there alone. She stood next to the car, the morning sun bouncing off her vibrant hair. "Good morning," she greeted him.

"Where's Tristan?" he asked, looking around. "Is he running late?"

Her face turned red. "He's taking the bus."

"Oh?"

"Yeah." She squirmed. "We sort of broke up."

"I'm sorry." And he actually was. He wondered if what he'd said to Tristan yesterday had had anything to do with it. Then again, Tristan and Rachel had been getting on each other's nerves for weeks.

Then the light hit the purple in Rachel's hair, and with her face turned slightly upward, she looked so perfect. Luke started to feel less sorry. Tristan and Rachel were over. Tristan wasn't Rachel's boyfriend anymore. And now Rachel was standing here with him.

Rachel shrugged. "Yeah, me too. But it was mutual. We just weren't a good match, and it took us a little while to figure it out."

"That sucks," he offered.

"Yeah." She leaned back against the car. "It had been building up for a long time. We just, I don't know, drove each other crazy." She laughed forcedly. "It was fun while it lasted, but you know . . ."

"Yeah." Luke nodded. "I'm still sorry, though." *Actually, not so much anymore.*

"Yeah, well . . ." She smiled up at him. "I guess it's for the best or whatever."

"Yeah. He was a pain in the ass, anyway," Luke joked.

"Don't say that," she said. "He's great—we just . . . didn't work."

She was right. Luke made a mental note to apologize to Tristan later. For a lot of things. "Okay. Sorry."

"You should be," she reprimanded him lightly.

"Maybe after this whole thing is over, you'll let me take you out to dinner to apologize fully," he teased, only half kidding.

Her face clouded. "Luke . . ." She looked away.

"What? What did I do?"

"No, it's just . . . So many things are different now, and . . . I don't know." She opened the door of the car. "Let's just go to the courthouse."

He stared uncomprehendingly at her. "I don't understand. What things are different?"

"Can we just go?"

"No," he said. "Hang on. Are you saying you just don't like me anymore?" As soon as the words were out there, he felt embarrassed.

"God, Luke!" Rachel's eyes flashed. "You couldn't even hang on two seconds! What were you doing, waiting around for Tristan and me to break up so you could 'make your move'? God!"

"It wasn't like that!" Luke argued.

She shook her head. "Whatever. It doesn't matter, anyway. Because we've all changed so much since everything happened, and I just don't think you and I would get along that way."

"Changed? What changed?"

"You!" she burst out. "You're the one who changed! I thought you were this great guy and then all this stuff happened and you just *changed!*"

Luke stepped back, shocked. "What are you talking about?"

"I feel like I don't even know you anymore," she told him. "You are a mess right now, okay? You're obsessed. This trial, it's all you talk about, all you think about." She started talking faster, picking up steam. "You're sullen and guarded, and sometimes you're just outright mean!"

"Hey!" Luke protested. "I—"

"You *punched* Drew! In the *face!*"

"That was—"

"You swear like crazy; it's impossible to even talk to you anymore!"

"Plenty of people swear!"

"And all of a sudden you're hanging out with Cooper Albright?"

"How do you know—?" Luke spluttered. "I didn't take anything from him!"

Rachel paused, catching her breath. Her face was red and

angry. "You aren't who I thought you were," she said quietly, accusingly.

"Well, I'm sorry I'm not perfect. But this whole thing's been *just a little* hard for me," he spat back.

"Yeah, well, you never should have been there that night, anyway," she told him.

"Hey. Don't blame me for this. I didn't kill Russell."

She exhaled sharply. "No. But you didn't save him either."

He didn't respond. He didn't know how.

CHAPTER 48

THE WAITING ROOM inside the courthouse seemed larger with only half as many occupants as there'd been the day before. Luke sat alone and waited until the bailiff came to get him. He entered the courtroom slowly, heading toward the witness stand with a jostled feeling in his stomach. He saw Rachel, sitting alone and tossing him an encouraging sort of smile. He saw Tristan a few rows back, watching Luke nervously. Two people who must have been Russell's parents were seated behind the district attorney. He recognized the Applegates, dressed formally, sitting behind Hayden.

As Luke passed the defendant's table, he caught Hayden's eye for a split second. Hayden's face was pleading. There was no trace now of the coldness Luke had seen in the jail. For a second, it was just Hayden. Luke's best friend.

Luke remembered a day, junior year, when he and Hayden had cut class and gone down to the Grill. They'd taken Hayden's car. It was right after Hayden's parents had bought it for him. Luke had been admiring it, saying all the things he thought he should. He'd complimented the speed, the look, how it handled. And Hayden had just stood there, silent. Luke had known something was wrong. He'd asked Hayden, and Hayden had given him this look, this pleading look, exactly like the one in the courtroom. But it was only for a moment, and then Hayden was himself again, telling Luke that he was just fine.

Why couldn't Hayden ever just talk to me? Maybe I could have helped him. Then again, I never really confided in him either. What kind of friends were we?

One of the wooden legs of the chair on the witness stand was shorter than the others, and the chair rocked slightly as Luke sat down. It took him a second to settle into the seat, and when that was accomplished, he twisted so he was facing Hayden's lawyer. *Stop stalling. It won't help.*

"Do you swear to tell the truth, the whole truth, and nothing but the truth, so help you God?" he was asked.

"I do," he said, and it began.

"Please state your name for the record," said Martin Barnes, attorney-at-law.

"Lucas William Prescott." Even his name sounded wrong.

"What is your relationship to the defendant?"

Luke looked Hayden in the eye. "He's my best friend," Luke said, his gaze never breaking from Hayden's.

"And on the night of February the third, you accompanied the defendant and the deceased up onto the cliff over Briar Lake, is that correct?"

"Yes." *Just stick to the truth, Luke. Just tell the truth and everything will be okay.*

"What was your relationship with the deceased?"

The deceased. "We were never friends. But we weren't, like, enemies. We didn't really talk much."

"Would it be fair to say that you had no *strong* feelings of liking or disliking toward Russell Conrad?"

"Yeah. Um, yes." Formal speech was slipping from him.

"And what happened on the cliff, Mr. Prescott?"

"Well, Russell and Hayden, they had an argument."

"What was the argument about?"

Luke's memory ground into motion. "Russell said something about Nicole to get a rise out of Hayden. That's why they were arguing. And then Hayden pushed him."

"What happened next?" Martin Barnes looked Luke in the eye, and Luke suddenly understood the position that the lawyer was in. Luke had refused to speak to Mr. Barnes about his testimony, so the man had absolutely no idea what Luke was going to say. With each question, Mr. Barnes was putting Hayden's future on the line.

Luke chose his words with the utmost care. "Russell tripped." *That's true.* "The cliff was rocky." *It was.* "And then Russell went off the cliff. Hayden and I ran down to the bank. I went into the water and got Russell. Hayden helped me pull him out of the lake. Hayden called 911 and then I tried CPR."

"Mr. Prescott," Mr. Barnes said slowly, "during the whole ordeal, did Mr. Applegate show concern for Russell Conrad's well-being?"

I'm not sure. But Luke couldn't say that. It would sound like a no. And Luke wasn't sure yet if he wanted to say no. "After we pulled him out of the lake, Hayden said, 'He's not breathing!' He was . . . terrified." *Good. It's the truth, but it's not really an answer, is it?*

Martin Barnes smiled at Luke. "No further questions."

When Angela Garvey stood up, Luke fought the urge to turn and run. He wanted to flee down the aisle and out the heavy wooden doors of the courtroom. *Would the security guards stop me? Would they drag me kicking and screaming back to the witness stand?*

"Mr. Prescott, you have previously said that you think of the defendant as your best friend."

"Yep. Er, yeah. I mean, yes." *Shit, shit, shit.*

"So would it be a fair statement that your answers as an eyewitness would be biased by this relationship?"

She's not sure what I'm going to say either. She's trying to cover her bases, Luke realized. "I've been sworn in," he said defensively. "I said I would tell the truth. And I will."

The district attorney nodded. "Excellent. So. Why were the three of you on the cliff the night of Russell Conrad's death?"

"There's this initiation thing that the fencing team does at Briar, which is basically that when you make the varsity team, you have to jump off the cliff, and Briar Lake runs right underneath, so you land in the water, and Russell was there because he'd just made the team and he was going to jump, and Hayden's a captain, so he was there, and I was there to watch, too, because I'm on varsity, too." *Was that all one sentence?*

"Thank you," Angela Garvey said curtly. "Mr. Applegate is not the only fencing captain of the boys' team, is he?"

"No, there's one other captain."

"A Mr. Ward McAfee," Ms. Garvey supplied.

"Yes."

"Why was it that the defendant accompanied Russell Conrad that night, and not Mr. McAfee?"

Luke frowned. "I don't know. It had to be one of them. Hayden volunteered."

"Did anyone suggest to Mr. Applegate that, considering the volatile nature of his relationship with Mr. Conrad, it might be better if the other fencing captain were to go to the cliff?"

Luke couldn't lie. He remembered the conversation he'd had in the dorm room. And he was under oath. "Yeah. I guess I did."

"But Mr. Applegate insisted," supplied Ms. Garvey.

"Well, I wouldn't say he insisted," Luke protested. *Damage control, damage control.* "He just, I mean, he'd already volunteered, and he didn't want to back out."

"How honorable," Ms. Garvey commented.

"Objection!" called Mr. Barnes from across the room.

"Withdrawn," the district attorney said quickly. "You have already said that the defendant pushed Mr. Conrad up on the cliff."

"Yes."

"And you have said that Russell Conrad fell off the cliff afterward."

"Yes."

"Mr. Prescott, as the only eyewitness to Russell Conrad's death, would you say that Hayden Applegate is responsible for the death of Russell Conrad?"

Headmaster Grunberg had told him that when the time came, Luke would know what to say. Clearly, the old man could not have been more wrong. He had no idea what to say. Everyone was staring at him. Luke met Hayden's eyes across the courtroom. His friend was sitting hunched over at the defense's table, his hands resting in his lap, his face impassive. In that moment, Luke realized that he would never know what Hayden had intended when he pushed Russell. He would never know whether Hayden had meant to kill Russell or had merely lashed out in a moment of anger. He would never know if his friend was a murderer. But that wasn't the question. The question was one of responsibility.

Hayden had climbed up a cliff with a boy he despised. Hayden had argued with that boy on the cliff. In a moment of anger, Hayden had reached out and shoved that boy. That boy had fallen to his death. But Luke had also gone to the cliff that night. There were so many things he could have done differently. That he should have done differently. He should have stepped in between Russell and Hayden on the cliff. He should have stopped them from arguing in the first place. He should have insisted that Ward go to the cliff with Russell instead of Hayden and himself. He should have said at the team meeting that Russell shouldn't have to jump. But he hadn't done any of that. Instead, he'd just gone along with what Hayden had wanted. And now Russell was dead.

When it came down to it, it didn't matter that Hayden was the one who'd pushed. What mattered was that none of them should have been there that night. Luke had gone up on the cliff. So had Hayden. So had Russell. It had been stupid and dangerous, but they had chosen to be there, and from the moment that choice had been made, the responsibility for what happened became theirs. They were all three victims, and they were all three culprits. Russell wasn't there to take his share of the blame, but Luke was. Hayden did not belong at that table alone.

Sitting on the witness stand, with everyone's eyes on him, Luke thought about the bad choices he'd made that night on the cliff. He thought about the bad choices that he'd made since. He thought about Tristan and Rachel, the only people who'd stuck by him. He thought about the way he'd treated them. He'd been friends with Tristan to get to Rachel, and he'd been friends with Rachel because he'd wanted her. They had been there for him, and he had taken advantage of that.

Luke looked around the courtroom. He saw Hayden, shifting nervously in his chair, and in that instant he forgave his friend. It wasn't Hayden who had put Luke in this terrible position. Luke had put himself there. He looked at Rachel and at Tristan, sitting several rows apart. He hoped that they would forgive him for the kind of friend he'd been. He hoped that he would one day be worthy of their friendship.

Rachel's right, he thought. *I am a mess.* Luke looked at Hayden's mother, sitting behind her son with her hands clasped together, her left hand up by her throat, fiddling with the pearls around her neck. She reminded Luke a little of his own mother. Luke wondered what it would have been like if she had come to the courthouse with him. He tried to picture her there, smiling supportively at him from the front row. *She was a mess, too,* Luke considered, processing this new thought slowly. *What happened with Dad wrecked her as much as this wrecked me. Maybe it doesn't excuse the things she did, but maybe it doesn't have to. If I want people to forgive me for what I've done, how can I not forgive her?*

Then, finally, Luke thought of his father, and for the first time in years, he let himself see what had always been right in front of him. That Jack Prescott had not been weak. Jack Prescott had not been selfish. Jack Prescott had been sick. Though he'd loved his family very much, he had succumbed to mental illness and he had ended his own life. And it was time Luke stopped hating him for it.

Luke couldn't change his past, but he could change his future. He could take control of his life. He could do the right thing in this moment. It was time that someone stepped up.

The district attorney coughed impatiently into her hand. "Answer the question, Mr. Prescott," she demanded. "Was Hayden Applegate responsible for the death of Russell Conrad?"

Luke took a deep breath and straightened his back. "No," he said, looking her straight in the eye. "We both were."

THE FOLLOWING DAY, Hayden Applegate testified in his own defense. On the stand, he broke down and cried, begging for forgiveness for not being able to stop the terrible accident. During his testimony, he looked each juror in the eye, and his voice caught on his words so many times that the judge had to ask him repeatedly if he was able to continue. Three days later, Hayden Applegate was declared not guilty of the murder of Russell Conrad.

Luke Prescott was not present.

ACKNOWLEDGMENTS

First and foremost, I want to thank my family for the help they gave me while I was writing this book. My mother, Emily Anhalt, read every chapter as soon as I finished it, and her enthusiasm motivated me to keep writing. My father, Eduardo Anhalt, provided me with endless encouragement and tried valiantly (but usually unsuccessfully) to keep me sane during the more stressful aspects of the process. I would also like to thank my inspiring grandparents—Marilyn Katz, George Petty, and Nedda Anhalt—for all their wise advice. I am grateful to my sister, Erica Anhalt, and my cousin Margie Lynn for their encouragement. I am also grateful to my uncle and aunt, Jimmy and Dena Katz, for their support, for the photos, and for not letting me freeze to death in Central Park.

I am greatly indebted to Christiane Jacox, Kathy Neustadt, Emma Kennelly, and Emily Shaw, who read and gave me feedback on early drafts of this novel. I am extremely thankful to Nikki Van De Car and Laurie Liss at Sterling Lord Literistic for their perceptive help in refining the story and their kind guidance as it became a book. I also want to thank Julie Tibbott at Houghton Mifflin Harcourt for helping me to turn *Freefall* into a much better novel than the one I originally sent her. Finally, I want to thank Eric Swanson for helping me decorate Luke's room, and the Hopkins School fencing team and the Dartmouth College fencing club for showing me that the pen is only a little bit mightier than the sword.